MATTHEW J. PALLAMARY

CyberChrist

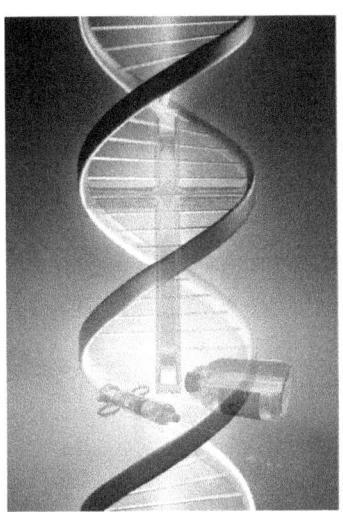

by

Matthew J. Pallamary

Mystic Ink Publishing

MATTHEW J. PALLAMARY

Mystic Ink Publishing
San Diego, CA
www.mysticinkpublishing.com

ISBN 10: 0692240985 (sc)
ISBN 13: 978-0692240984 (sc)
Printed in the United States of America
San Bernardino, California

This book is printed on acid-free paper made from 30% post-consumer waste recycled material.

Library of Congress Control Number: 2014911632

Book Jacket and Page Design: Matthew J. Pallamary/San Diego CA
Author's Photograph: Matthew J. Pallamary -- Gibbs Photo/Malibu CA

DEDICATION

This book is dedicated to Colleen Kennedy.

CHAPTER ONE

Ashley Butler set her chamomile tea and bran muffin down on her desk and hit the power button on her computer. While the little electronic monster under her desk beeped and chattered to life, she brushed ringlets of long brown hair from her face and pulled them into a pony tail, then she leaned back in her chair and watched the never-ending activity from The San Diego Times newsroom through the tinted glass wall of her office.

Mounted close to the ceiling above the doors, half a dozen TV monitors lined the far wall showing CNN, MSNBC, local, and national news. Smaller computer screens glowed from rows of cubicles below them. The steady clicking of keyboards filled the air while phones rang and people scurried in and out of offices.

Less than a year ago Ashley had occupied one of those cubicles until her prize winning story about the murder of an environmental terrorist brought her from reporter to feature writer. Her editor and mentor Scott Miller had worked through the assignment with her, pushing for more revisions. His suggestions helped pull things together, sparking a close father-daughter relationship that made her eager to please by giving him nothing but her best work.

Her computer played the opening strains of Virginia Woolf by the Indigo Girls, signaling the log-on screen. Ashley nibbled her muffin and tapped in her password with one hand. Her email popped up showing seventeen messages. She recognized sixteen of the names. She had never seen the seventeenth. It had an enclosure.

Dr. Justin Stephens -- Subject: **Immortality**

"What's that all about?" she muttered, double clicking the mail icon. The message screen appeared, but it had no words. She clicked on the enclosure. Pictures and algebraic equations filled her screen.

The first picture showed a wizened sexless countenance with wrinkled, ashen skin, no eyebrows, and a bald head that seemed too large for such a small face. A beaked nose and receding chin looked as if the mouth would swallow them. Jagged teeth sprouted from red gums and milky blue eyes protruded under lashless eyelids.

Ashley's breath hitched when she read the caption beneath it.

> Diagnosis/Prognosis: Chris Daniels, age 14 presents with Progeria, an acceleration of the aging process to approximately seven times the normal rate. Symptoms include heart disease, arteriosclerosis, arthritis, stunted growth, and premature aging. Applied gene therapy has resulted in the isolation and turning off of an inverted insertion in the long arm of chromosome one. The miraculous results of the administered protocol are shown in the following photos.

More pictures followed, their sequence appearing to go backward in time. In the second picture, Chris's eyes looked clearer. His or her skin appeared softer with a flush of color; as if it now held moisture, and the child's teeth had evened some. Ashley thought she saw peach fuzz where eyebrows should be.

The child's face looked fuller and more feminine in the third picture and the teeth looked straighter. Ashley saw hair on Chris's head and the kid definitely had eyebrows. The fire in Chris's now ice blue eyes burned brighter.

The two pictures that followed looked younger and more perfect somehow; androgynous with brighter eyes, a normally proportioned face, and fully formed eyebrows. Feathery lashes, a thickening head of long hair, and healthy skin tone accented everything else, giving Chris an angelic countenance.

I've seen this trick before, Ashley thought. They Photo-shopped these to make it look like the person ages at warp speed.

In the last picture, Chris's hair had grown down to his or her shoulders. Other than tiny crow's feet around the kid's eyes and indeterminate sex, Chris looked like a normal teenager, only this kid was beautiful. Ashley couldn't believe the caption under the picture.

Chris Daniels – Age:17

She read the accompanying text with mounting confusion.

I have risked my life and endangered yours by sending this, but I have no choice. In my studies of the genes associated with Progeria, I discovered how to turn off those tied to aging, making the cells in Chris's body regenerate. All of my data indicate that this process will continue, eventually regenerating every single one of Chris's cells. Chris has gone from a short-lived blip on the sea of life to the genetic equivalent of the fountain of youth.

Unfortunately, as a result of my discovery, three doctors, five interns, and three support staff have disappeared, most of them right from Genengineering in the middle of the day. Now my life and Chris's are in danger.

I realize how crazy and melodramatic this sounds, but the government has seized my lab, my research, and my proof. I fear that my entire staff has been silenced forever. My only saving grace is the backup of my work that I kept off site.

Please be discreet in your inquiries, but I urge you to look into what happened to Genengineering at 1022 Sorrento Valley Road, then talk to Dr. Russell Holmstedt. His address is 4458 Bird Rock Ave. in La Jolla. Russ has proof that will verify my claim. Tell him Justin sent you for Methuselah. He'll understand. Be careful. No one knows what he has, but they could be watching.

I will contact you at my first opportunity.

Sincerely,
Dr. Justin Stephens, Ph.D.

Ashley felt a chill when she googled Dr. Holmstedt and found the La Jolla address Stephens had given her. She googled Genengineering and received the following message.

THE PAGE CANNOT BE FOUND

THE PAGE YOU ARE LOOKING FOR MIGHT HAVE BEEN REMOVED, HAD ITS NAME CHANGED, OR IS TEMPORARILY UNAVAILABLE.

Further down the page it said:

HTTP 404 – FILE NOT FOUND
INTERNET INFORMATION SERVICES

She pulled out the White Pages and found a listing.   Picking up the phone, she punched in the number. After two rings, a recording came on the line.

"We're sorry. The number you have reached has been disconnected. If you feel you have dialed in error, please hang up and try again."

She did. Same recording. No forwarding number. She tried Holmstedt's. Same message. She set the phone down and stared at her reflection in the tinted glass trying to imagine what it would be like to be immortal, then she scrolled through the pictures again. Chris looked too perfect. This had to be a hoax.

After reading the letter a second time, Ashley forwarded it to some friends and co-workers, wondering what their reactions would be. The fact that Genengineering and Holmstedt were both listed and now disconnected made her uneasy. More minds would give her a reality check, and right now she needed one.

After answering the rest of her e-mail, Ashley thought about her feature on human rights abuses at the Mexican border. She had to make a noon deadline. Gathering her notes from the latest rape victim's husband, she checked his statement. Another half a page and she'd be done.

Her phone rang halfway through the last sentence. She hurried to finish before snatching up the handset.

"Ashley Butler."

"Hi Ash, its Scott. I'll spring for lunch if you'll tell me about that crazy email you sent."

"Deal. Come on down and get me." She hung up and pulled out her compact to check her makeup, then gazed into her own brown eyes, struck by the deepening laugh lines at their corners. Immortality, she thought. Wouldn't that be something?

She looked up from letting her hair down to see Scott coming toward her office. He wore a denim work shirt and faded jeans. A few inches taller than her five eight, he had an easy smile, shaggy, gray-streaked hair, and eyes that matched the blue of his shirt. He nodded to people as he passed cubicles, gliding in his laid back surfer's gait. She found herself smiling by the time he popped his head in the door.

"Ready?" He held the door open, talking as she stepped through. "Someone spent a lot of time making those pictures look like that kid aged backward."

"Looks convincing, huh?"

"You'll fire up all the online kooks if that one gets out."

They went through the double doors on the far side of the news room, passing under the monitors when she heard the name "Russell Holmstedt" above the other voices. She whirled, bumping into Scott.

"What's the matter?" he said, surprised.

She held her hand up and heard the name again from above. Looking up at the monitor, she saw a dark-haired male announcer.

"Noted gerontologist and National Science Academy award winner, Russell Holmstedt was found dead in his home this morning from an apparent heart attack."

A picture of a sandy haired, middle-aged, bearded man wearing wire-rimmed glasses filled the screen behind the announcer.

"Holmstedt, known for his groundbreaking work in recombinant DNA techniques was thought to be in good health, with no preexisting heart conditions. Funeral arrangements are pending."

"Holmstedt?" Scott said, rousing her from her confusion. "Why does that sound familiar?"

Ashley forced herself to breathe. "The email." She found it hard to think. "I tried calling his number."

"And?"

"Out of service. Genengineering too."

Scott ran his fingers through his graying hair and his eyes took on a far away look. "Guy had a heart attack. You saw his picture. He's my age."

"Noted gerontologist and National Science Academy award winner," Ashley said.

Scott took her arm and started for the door. "Let's talk about it over *fajitas*."

Ashley pulled away, walking faster. "I have to take a rain check," she called back.

Scott hurried to catch up to her.

"I want to verify the addresses," she said, rummaging through her purse.

Scott grinned and shook his head. "I'll come with you."

She pulled her cell phone from her purse and held it up. "I have my life line right here. If I need you I'll sound the alarm."

Scott held the door open, letting Ashley go.

CHAPTER TWO

Ashley drove her Prius down Sorrento Valley Road checking addresses until she found a small one story mirrored building with an empty parking lot and no sign at number 1022. Dusty reflective glass surrounded a clean spot above the entrance where a sign had been. Ashley saw the outlines of letters that spelled:

GENENGINEERING

She parked in front, killed the engine and put her hand on the door handle, stopping when she realized her hands shook. Silly, she thought, closing her eyes. She took a long slow breath before stepping out of the car. Hurrying to the front door, she pressed her face to the window. A pile of broken sheet rock littered the floor. Conduit, wires, fixtures, and heating ducts hung from the ceiling. No sign of activity. Nothing to be afraid of.

Ashley felt like some unseen weight lifted from her when she left the parking lot. She drove south on I-5 to Pacific Beach where she found a parking space across the street from 4458 Bird Rock Ave. The doors to the sprawling, split-level ranch house had been sealed with black and yellow coroner's tape. The name on the mailbox said Holmstedt.

Feeling the shakes again coupled with the sense of being a trespasser, Ashley strode purposefully to the front door and peered in through the window where she saw a couch, easy chairs, a big screen television, and southwestern Indian art on the walls. Nothing looked out of place, which only added to her uneasiness. No need to stay here any longer, she thought breathing deep to calm her racing heart. She turned to leave and collided with a man, scaring herself even more with her own short scream.

"Who are you?" she gasped, backing away with her hand pressed to her thumping heart.

He stared for a long uncomfortable moment before his hand went to the pocket of his dark suit, coming back out with a wallet. He flipped it open revealing a gold badge and ID. His eyes never left hers.

Federal Marshall Jon Mossbarger.

Ashley looked past the wallet to a balding man with a hard pockmarked face and dark questioning eyes that showed no emotion. She'd seen guys like this before. All cop.

"What are you doing here?" he said evenly.

She found it hard to swallow. "Following up on a story." She fumbled her press card from her purse. "Ashley Butler, San Diego Times."

He glanced at her card and waved it away. "What kind of story?"

"A profile," she said, winging it. "Dr. Holmstedt was a National Science Academy award winner."

His stare never wavered. "Is that why you were snooping around that building in Sorrento Valley?"

Her breath caught. How did he know that? "I wasn't snooping!"

Mossbarger showed no reaction.

"I was following a lead."

"Where did you get it?"

His directness made her self-conscious. "None of your business," she snapped, instantly wishing she hadn't.

To her surprise, his face relaxed. "Listen," he said, holding up his hands. "You're doing a story on the doctor? That's great. Can't wait to read it."

His sudden change scared her. "If you'll excuse me I have to go. I am under a deadline."

"When are they going to run it?"

"Don't know yet." She stepped around him.

"I'll be watching for it," he said as she passed.

Ashley didn't look back.

Forty-five minutes later, she walked into the county courthouse downtown San Diego where she found no records, birth or otherwise for Chris Daniels, and no record of Dr. Stephens. She also came up empty in her search for any tax records for Genengineering. The same for building or sign permits, business licenses, deeds, or lawsuits. Officially, none of it existed.

Driving back to the Times, she tried to make sense of it. The letter outlines on the building at the Sorrento Valley address showed something had been there. She shook off a chill when she thought of how Dr. Holmstedt had died before she could talk to him. Then there was that creep Mossbarger. Cop. Her stomach flip-flopped. How could a high-tech business in Sorrento Valley have no records?

Ashley parked at the *Times* and took the elevator upstairs where she hurried through the newsroom, anxious to get to her office. Her heart sank when she found Scott there reading a search warrant while Mossbarger and a gawky kid with glasses loaded her computer onto a cart.

"What do you think you're doing?" she said, rushing toward Mossbarger.

Scott grabbed her arm and the kid backed away, wide-eyed.

"It's in the warrant," Mossbarger said. "Your computer is being confiscated as evidence. We have reason to believe it's connected to a crime."

"What?"

"Sorry. You're going to have to come with us too."

She shook, wanting to strangle him. Scott's arm came around her shoulders. He picked up her phone and punched in a number, calling over his shoulder to Mossbarger, "She's not going anywhere without a lawyer. Hey, Jeff," he said into the phone. "I need you down in Ashley's office right now. Some Feds are walking off with her computer." Keeping his gaze steady on Mossbarger, he disconnected and punched in another number. "Hi, Rob. I need another computer hooked up in Ashley's office ASAP. She's got a hell of a first amendment story."

CHAPTER THREE

A shley dropped into her chair with her purse in her lap to wait for their lawyer, forcing herself to breathe deep to calm herself. The gawky kid crossed his arms and took a seat on the far side of the room. Every time she glanced in his direction he looked away. Ashley rolled her chair closer to the desk and slipped a pad and pen from her purse. Opening the pad on her lap, she put pen to paper and looked up to see Mossbarger looking at her.

"What is it you're charging her with?" Scott said.

Mossbarger turned back to him. "Did I say we were charging her?"

"You're not? Then she doesn't have to go."

Ashley scribbled on her pad while Scott kept Mossbarger's attention.

> Scott,
>
> Send that e-mail with the Dorian Gray pix to everyone
> you can trust and tell them to do the same.

"Look paper boy," Mossbarger said, flourishing a sheaf of documents. "I got a warrant. You want an IRS seizure? I'll lock this rag down so tight, you won't know a classified ad from a health permit."

"Go ahead and try you bureaucratic pissant," someone said from the hallway.

Mossbarger's face darkened.

Ashley's heart lifted, recognizing the voice of the paper's chief council. Once Jeff Hamilton sank his teeth into something he hung onto it like a pit bull.

Hamilton came through the door taking everything in before zeroing in on Mossbarger. Recognizing his opponent, he crossed the room, sticking a business card in Mossbarger's face when he reached him. Mossbarger pushed it away and the two stood eye to eye.

Jeff's short black hair stood on end like an agitated cat and his eyes looked bugged out as if his body needed every outlet for the energy that charged through him. He always looked this way, even when calm. When Mossbarger didn't respond, Jeff nodded to Ashley, acknowledged Scott, and glared back at Mossbarger. While the two faced off, Ashley folded the note and tucked it between her thumb and palm.

"You try that IRS shit around here," Jeff said, "and every paper from the *New York Times* to the *Podunk Bugle* and all the wire services in between will be doing their own feature investigations into first amendment abuses." He turned from Mossbarger and winked at Ashley. "You want that?"

"I don't want to talk about it here," Mossbarger said, not moving as if proving that he had given no ground. "It's a matter of national security. We need Miss Butler to come downtown. Here's the subpoena." He handed a paper to Jeff, who scanned it before giving it back.

"You ready to answer a few questions for junior G-man, Ashley?"

"Whatever you tell me to do, that's what I'm doing." She felt her anxiety up itself a notch.

"All right." Jeff held out his hand. "Let's get this shit over with."

She grabbed her purse, stood and gave Scott a hug, sliding the note into his back pocket.

"Don't worry about me," she said, walking out the door flanked by Mossbarger and Hamilton. Mossbarger's geek flunky followed, pulling Ashley's computer behind him on a hand cart.

Once in the parking lot, the kid disappeared into a van with her computer. Mossbarger insisted on driving them in his government issue Ford. Ashley expected a million questions on the ride downtown, but Mossbarger stayed quiet.

He brought them to a spacious office on the second floor of a federal building downtown. A large mahogany desk filled the center of the room, set off from paneled walls by a thick earth-toned carpet. Rows of leather bound volumes lined a bookshelf on one wall, reminding Ashley of her grandfather's den. All it needed was a moose head. Mossbarger gestured toward a pair of high-backed chairs in front of the desk.

"He'll be here in a minute," he said.

"Who?" Hamilton asked, sitting down in one of the chairs.

"Ken Dawson, Director of West Coast Operations."

Jeff pulled a legal pad and pen from his brief case. "West coast operations of what?"

As if on cue, a stoic looking older man came into the room through a door on the far side. Silver-haired with probing blue eyes, he looked trim and in good physical shape. His tailored suit, shined shoes, tie clasp, and silk tie spoke of a man who paid attention to detail.

"Ken Dawson." He extended his hand to Jeff, then to Ashley, giving a firm handshake. "Thank you for coming down," he said going around the desk. "Sorry about the abruptness, but time is of the essence." He settled into a leather chair behind the desk. Mossbarger stood by the door behind them. Not being able to see him sent a creepy tickling down the back of Ashley's neck.

"What the hell is going on here?" she said.

"Dr. Justin Stephens," Dawson said, fixing her with a steady gaze.

She shrugged.

"The one who emailed you the pictures of the kid," Mossbarger said from behind her.

"How did you know that?"

Dawson held a hand up. "It was sent from a government facility." He eyed Ashley again. "We traced it to you, then you showed up at his old lab and his deceased partner's house. Of course we wanted to talk to you."

"Stephens sent me an email," Ashley said. "So what? Lots of people send me email."

Dawson nodded emphatically. "I'm sure you're not involved in any criminal activity, but the man who emailed you is. We're hoping you can help us catch him."

The tension inside her relaxed a notch, but she still felt defensive. "Help you?" She looked over at Hamilton who shook his head no.

"Let me tell you a story," Dawson said. "You can decide for yourself."

Jeff set his pen down on his pad, folded his arms, and leaned back, crossing his legs.

Ashley settled deeper into her chair. "I'm all ears."

"Dr. Stephens started out as a dedicated researcher who devoted his life to finding a cure for a rare genetic disease called Progeria." Dawson looked to Jeff, then to Ashley, letting the weight of his gaze settle on her.

"He sounds like a real humanitarian," Jeff said, then with more emphasis. "How could a guy like that go bad?"

"In the past six or seven years he's had numerous grants," Dawson said, showing no reaction to Jeff's question. "He worked long days and only took breaks to present papers at conferences, driving himself harder and harder until he ended up strung out on amphetamines."

"Then he lost the line between reality and fantasy," Mossbarger said from behind, startling Ashley. "Now he thinks he can make people live forever. He's stolen sensitive government data and funds from research grants, then he kidnapped one of his patients and murdered his partner."

"Murdered?" Ashley said in disbelief.

"Stephens has an unlimited supply of drugs," Dawson continued, "and his demands get more irrational with each passing day."

Ashley strained to keep the thread of credibility intact in her mind. "He's that far gone?"

Dawson leaned back in his chair, steepling his fingers. "Stephens believes he has power over death. Does that sound like a stable individual?"

Ashley had to admit, the immortality claim didn't sound sane, but this story didn't sound too kosher either.

"We're afraid of what Stephens might do to the kid," Mossbarger said.

Jeff stood. "Not to mention how bad this could make the government look. I'm sure you have some concern for your secrets and missing grant money."

"I'm not going to lie and say we don't," Dawson said, leveling his gaze at Jeff.

Jeff stuffed his pad into his briefcase. "You took Ashley's computer. What do you want with us?"

Mossbarger came around and perched on the edge of Dawson's desk. "We want to know if Stephens tries to contact you again."

"And please." Dawson's eyes implored. "I know we're asking a lot and I know this goes against your instincts, but I have to ask you not to run a story. Stephens is a walking time bomb. If he sees anything in the paper it could set him off."

"You expect us to sit on this?" Ashley said. "After what you've done?"

Dawson ran a hand through his silvery hair and sighed. "A few days are all we ask. A little time so we can track him down. If you work with us, we'll give you an exclusive."

"And if we don't?" Jeff said.

"I can make your life difficult." Mossbarger stood.

"Enough of that." Dawson said, cutting him off with an edge in his voice. "Listen, Miss Butler," he said, softening. "The child's life is in danger. Give us a little time."

"We'll be talking." Jeff started for the door. "Come on Ashley." He gestured for her to join him. She looked from Dawson to Mossbarger, then stood and walked to the door, surprised when neither of them objected.

"You going to give us a ride back to the paper?" Jeff said, over his shoulder. "Or are you going to make us take a cab?"

"Be there in a minute," Mossbarger said.

Once out in the hallway, Ashley asked. "What do you think?"

Jeff rested his hand on her shoulder. "They're full of shit."

CHAPTER FOUR

Mossbarger drove Ashley and Jeff back north on 163 through Balboa Park in silence, the same way he had brought them. Ashley watched the passing foliage with more questions than answers bubbling through her mind. She looked over at Jeff, who stared straight ahead.

In a matter of hours her life had gone from real and predictable to surreal and unbelievable, all from a single email. Killer doctor speed freak? Discoverer of immortality? Both unacceptable. What was really going on? Who were Mossbarger and Dawson? She shuddered, remembering the way they both looked at her. No – through her. She couldn't wait to hear Jeff's take on things and how he wanted to handle them.

Mossbarger took an exit and drove a few blocks to the *Times* where he turned into the paper's parking lot and dropped them at the front door.

"You'll hear from us in a couple of days," he said, putting the car into park. His eyes found Ashley's from the rear view mirror. "We're counting on you to keep quiet so we can catch this guy. Then you can have a field day." He winked.

Jeff grabbed his door handle and stepped out without speaking. Ashley followed. Both doors slammed on the same beat and the government issue Ford took off with a chirp from the rear tires.

"What should we do?" Ashley asked, falling into step beside Jeff. It felt good to be away from Mossbarger.

"Give me what you have so far and I'll get a P.I. to do some checking," Jeff said. "Nothing any of these G-men said makes any sense, that's for sure. We need to dig fast. Something really stinks here."

Ashley's heart beat faster. "Mossbarger definitely gives me the willies."

"His boss scares me more."

Ashley nodded. "I hear you. I did a standard records check and came up with zip, just like the email said." She hugged herself. If anything anyone has said has any truth to it…"

Jeff stopped and put his hand on her shoulder. "You lay low and let me handle this." He looked her in the eye. "Don't say or do anything until you hear from me, got it?"

"Don't leave me hanging."

Jeff smiled for the first time that day. "You ever know me to not follow through?"

"Good point."

Ashley thanked him and hurried back to her office where she saw someone at her desk. What now? She wondered.

"Son-of-a-bitch," she heard from out in the newsroom, recognizing Rob Gubala, their network admin's voice.

"It's doctor Demento," she said, coming through the door. "Fixed yet?"

Rob looked up from a keyboard, his brown eyes scowling under bushy eyebrows behind John Lennon granny glasses. His wispy goatee stood out on an angular face that looked even thinner because of the way he kept his sandy brown hair tied back in a pony tail. She saw from the Peace symbol on the CPU that her computer had been returned. "That was quick."

"They slicked your hard drive."

"They what?"

"Wiped all the data from it."

"Why in the hell would they do that?"

"They take all your data so they can track everything you do or have done so they know everything about you and everyone you know, then they obliterate any traces of what they consider 'critical to national security'. Wiping the drive is totally unnecessary, but it is their anal retentive standard operating procedure and their special way of saying 'fuck you'."

"What about backups?"

Rob pointed to her monitor, motioning with his head for her to come closer. "Anything you did today is lost, but I'll have you back online shortly." He looked up at the ceiling, then scanned the walls and desk. After checking the door, he let her take his place in front of the computer, pointing to what he had typed.

I don't mean to sound paranoid, but I think your office is bugged and your phone is tapped. Not only did they slick your drive, they got through our firewall and deleted your email account so they have access to our network. Don't trust any electronic channels of communication.

"Let me know if you need anything else," he said, narrowing his eyes. "I'll have your backups restored before the day's out."

She started typing.

Meet me in the parking lot in an hour.

He put his hand on Ashley's shoulder and gave it a reassuring squeeze. "See ya." He walked backward out the door, smiled, winked, and disappeared.

Spooked by Rob's behavior, Ashley grabbed a legal pad and wrote down everything she knew about Genengineering, Justin Stephens, Russell Holmstedt, and Chris Daniels, which didn't amount to much more than addresses and disconnected numbers. As soon as she finished she called Scott and told him to meet her in Jeff's office.

When she found Scott and Jeff waiting, she beckoned from the doorway for them to come. When they came out of the office, Ashley linked one arm with Scott's, took Jeff's with the other, and guided them to the end of the hall.

"They wiped all the data off of my hard drive and deleted my email account," she whispered. "Rob thinks my phone and office are bugged."

"Deleted your email from the server?" Scott said, incredulously.

"You might think Rob's paranoid," Ashley said, "but they got through our firewall and killed my account." She looked to Jeff. "If they bugged me, they probably bugged you too." She handed Jeff her notes. "You too Scott."

"We're not letting you out of our sight," Scott said.

"I'm going to meet Rob downstairs to talk about it."

Jeff stuffed Ashley's notes into his pocket. "I'll get someone working on this right away. Stay close, play stupid, and lay low. Let's see what we come up with before Mossbarger and Dawson come back with their next crock of shit."

"I'll have Rob configure you a laptop," Scott said, "so you can get your email and stay mobile."

"They'll see your mail before it ever gets to you," Jeff said.

"They can't stop me from sending it." She smiled for the first time since opening the message that morning. "What do you guys think? A fake? Some secret code?"

"I've been wondering about that myself," Scott said. "I've been reading it all morning while you two were with Elliot Ness."

"Dawson and Mossbarger say Stephens is a nutcase," Jeff said. "You ask me, those two are pretty strange themselves."

"And then there's a guy who conveniently died," Ashley said, looking from Jeff to Scott. "And a business that disappeared."

CHAPTER FIVE

Ashley found a FedEx mailer waiting for her on her chair back in her office. She looked over her shoulder, scanning the newsroom, half-expecting to see someone watching, but business went on with the usual bustle. She picked up the mailer, sat down in her chair and saw the return address.

J.S.
4458 Bird Rock Ave.
San Diego, CA 92121

After Mossbarger and Dawson's antics and the way Rob acted, she didn't feel safe here in her fishbowl office. Checking once more to make sure no one watched, she opened the mailer on her lap under the desk and found a flash drive. She slipped it into her purse and hurried downstairs to the underground parking lot to meet Rob.

After zig-zagging through the lot and driving in circles to make sure no one followed, Rob drove them West through Mission Valley on I-8 toward Ocean Beach. He checked his rear view mirrors before reaching into the back seat for a carrying case with a notebook computer in it.

"It's configured with phony email accounts," Rob said, setting it on Ashley's lap. "I don't trust anything on our network. On *any* network for that matter."

Ashley unzipped the case, flipped open the screen and hit the on switch. She looked over at Rob while the system booted. "You did good," she said, tapping the screen. "I really appreciate it. You're one of the only people I can trust."

"Those spooks scare the shit out of me." He pushed his glasses up on his nose. They went through our firewall like it wasn't there and deleted your account from a secure server. You can bet they have taps on every line coming into the building."

Ashley took the flash drive from her purse, popped it into one of the laptop's USB ports and started copying files to the hard drive. "Did you get a chance to look at the email I forwarded?" she asked while the files transferred.

Rob nodded.

"The guy who sent it is supposed to be strung out on amphetamines. They think he's going to kill the kid."

Rob made a dismissive gesture. "Those cops? You *know* they're lying."

She popped the drive from the port and showed it to Rob. "He just sent me a second installment."

"What are you waiting for? Let's check it out!"

"I have to salvage what's left of my story from the back ups so I don't miss my deadline. I'll look at the data later tonight when no one's around."

Rob drove to the end of the freeway where it turned onto Sunset Cliffs Boulevard. Ashley watched the passing palm trees, tennis courts, and baseball diamonds of Rob Field that marked the beginning of Ocean Beach. With lower rents compared to the upscale beaches of La Jolla and Del Mar, O.B. was a paradise to surfers and a mecca to people from the East coast.

Rob guided his Tesla into O.B. proper, where the sixties still kept a tenuous upper hand. Older buildings and strict zoning laws kept most of the developers out, but a few hard core money grubbers like Starbuck's and Jack in the Box had managed to run the independents off. Ashley had secured her place of honor in O.B.'s counterculture as one of four hundred of the original twelve hundred who finished the Great Peace March for Global Nuclear Disarmament.

Rob turned onto Newport Ave., past antique shops and weathered storefronts heading toward the beach. Another couple of blocks took them to Ashley's two room bungalow on Narragansett.

When she felt sure no one saw her, Ashley ran in and slid the laptop under her bed and hid the flash drive in one of her shoes. Satisfied that they were safe, she hurried back out to Rob, who checked his rear view mirrors before driving away.

"I've been thinking," he said, once they were back on Newport. "Those doctored pictures of the kid aren't what they seem. Maybe they put the kid's pictures in reverse or something. Whatever it is, I'm sure it's phony." He glanced over at her. "But there's a reason why those spooks want it so bad. I'm thinking there's something embedded in the message."

"If it was a put on," Ashley said. "It would explain why I can't find anything on Stephens or the kid, but I did see where the sign had been for Genengineering."

"I hate to sound like a conspiracy nut," Rob said, checking his rear view mirrors and both sides of them again, "but after what you told me about those Feds and the way they waltzed into our network, I'm sure it was a CIA or NSA front. I'm going to go through that email with a fine tooth decompiler." They pulled onto I-8 and headed toward Mission Valley.

"I have to go along with them for now," Ashley said. "They promised an exclusive if I played their game. Besides, I was dragged into the middle of this whether I like it or not."

Rob looked sideways at her. "Be careful, for Christ's sake. That Holmstedt guy had something they wanted. If they think you do..."

"That's why I plan on publishing what I find. If I play it right, anything happens to me, the Feds will end up with more people asking more questions than they want to answer."

Rob pulled onto an exit ramp. "I hope you're right."

After more circles and more mirror checks, Rob pulled his Tesla into the *Times* lot. They went into the building separately, Rob first to his lab, then Ashley to her office to work on her story.

A short time later, Rob called to tell her that all the data on her computer had been restored from backups, except the emails and the work she had done earlier that day, which meant she had to rewrite the last two pages of her story from memory. She threw herself into the task, finishing moments before Scott appeared in her doorway.

"Rob hasn't left the lab since you guys came back," he said, taking a seat on the edge of her desk. "Says he's run every scan and crypto program he knows of."

Ashley grabbed her jacket. "I need to get going." She motioned with her head for him to follow.

"Rob says that email is pure as the driven snow," Scott said, once they were out in the news room. "No code. No viruses. Straight document and graphics files. It is what it is."

"A hoax," Ashley said.

"Then why did the Feds erase it from your hard drive and the server?"

She started to answer, finding no words. Scott stayed silent a moment, then slapped himself on the forehead.

"What?"

"The code's in the message. Like an anagram or something."

"I have a flash drive from Stephens," Ashley whispered, once they were in the hall outside the newsroom. "I'm on my way home to look at it."

"I'll get the pizza." Scott pointed at her. "You provide the entertainment."

CHAPTER SIX

An hour and a half later, Scott sat at Ashley's kitchen table washing down the last piece of pizza with a sip of Corona. Ashley handed him another beer and refilled her wine glass before scooting her chair close to his so they could both see the notebook screen. She called up the document and she and Scott leaned forward to read what Justin Stephens had written.

Dear Miss Butler,

I heard about Holmstedt. It was wrong to involve him and I shouldn't have involved you, but I had nowhere else to turn. I know how fantastic my claims must sound, so I urge you to investigate them from a purely scientific perspective. You'll see that I speak the truth. I will not recommend an authority for you to verify my discovery with, so you cannot accuse me of having any complicity with what you discover.

Aside from my data, the only proof of this miracle is Chris, a child whose mutated genes doomed him to whither before he ever blossomed. Knowing he had a short life in a debilitated state made him bitter and full of rage. He thought of his short life as fleeting and meaningless.

Only the moment matters to Chris.

He's had three arrests for stolen cars and one for possession of marijuana. The police weren't fast enough to stop him from swallowing six doses of LSD.

Now that science has given him a reprieve from his death sentence, Chris has changed. The drugs, violence, and time in jail have made their mark, but I am convinced that a good heart lies beneath his anger.

The proof of my discovery and those who witnessed it have all been destroyed, but I have notes, formulas, and pictures of all the steps I took to sustain Chris's life beyond the wall of death. If I live through this I can replicate my results in a few short weeks. In the mean time I only have you to get my message out so the public is aware of what is happening. If the government silences us, the key to immortality will be lost.

They want me dead because I have discovered the secret of a gene that confers immortality. I introduced it into Chris's chromosomal DNA near chromosome #1, short arm, section 1, subsection 5.

The puzzle of implementing these cellular changes into Chris's deteriorating life processes plagued me for months until I realized that telomerase held the missing piece.

Telomeres are the protein-DNA structures at the ends of chromosomes that protect them from degradation, like the plastic tips they put on shoelaces. Telomerase loss causes chromosomal changes associated with cancer and aging. As cells deteriorate, telomeres grow shorter.

It is normally active only in stem cells as well as the cells that give rise to sperm and egg, however when cells become cancerous, telomerase is activated, which allows them to replicate endlessly.

Cancer cells can divide indefinitely in tissue culture if given adequate nutrients. Telomerase in normal cells are like a clock that is winding down, which is what we experience as aging.

Using monoclonal antibody production techniques,

I fused the modified aging cell to a stem cell, creating stem cell hybridomas. The stem cells produced blood cells fused with the telomere lengthening anti-aging genes.

These new genes integrated into the cell's chromosome, conferring immortality upon the cells they were cloned into and replicating new DNA in daughter progeny cells. The original cells died and the new immortal cells replaced them, essentially forming a new organism.

Chris's cells continued to incorporate the new DNA, replacing the mutated genes that aged him in the first place. I reinjected these into Chris's bones to multiply in vivo, creating daughter blood cells with the capability of producing the new gene product.

This process triggered high levels of growth hormone, which amplified and balanced the output from the hypothalamic-pituitary axis. The resulting homeostasis reversed the aging of the body's organ system. Ironically, the pattern that gave Chris eternal life is the same pattern that brings death by cancer.

Verify my claims with scientists of your own choosing. There is enough information in the files on the thumb drive that I sent you to support my claims. If you can save us, I can replicate my results.

Be wise and be careful.

Blessings,

Justin & Chris

CHAPTER SEVEN

Ashley stared at the algebraic formulas scrolling down the laptop's screen at the end of the letter, her mind buzzing with possibilities, every one of them too fantastic to consider and too evident to ignore. She couldn't believe Stephens' claim of discovering immortality and she couldn't trust anything Mossbarger or Dawson told her.

"Pretty far-fetched," Scott said, interrupting her thoughts.

She looked up, seeing the concern in his eyes. "Imagine, just for a minute," he said, pointing at the computer, "that this guy did discover immortality."

Feeling exposed with the letter up on the screen, Ashley closed the program, shut the notebook, and sat back with her arms crossed. "I don't know what to think."

Scott sighed. "Who would decide who lives?" he said. "Would life-prolonging treatments be restricted? Would people be allowed to live to a certain age? Would couples need breeding licenses? What if one partner grows tired of living and wants to die while their mate wants to go on?"

Ashley shook her head. "I'm sorry, but it's too far-fetched. I can't bring myself to believe it."

"I don't believe it either." Scott tapped the laptop. "But for shits and giggles, I have an old girlfriend who's a Ph.D. out at San Diego State. If anybody can make sense out of this genetic mumbo-jumbo, she can."

Ashley shrugged. "Can't hurt." She found another flash drive and copied the files for Scott. After the drive's light flashed, he popped it out and put it in the top pocket of his shirt. "I wonder if Jeff's having any luck."

"Be careful with that," Ashley said. "The way Mossbarger climbed out of the woodwork scares the hell out of me."

He patted his pocket. "It's safe. What about your copy?"

She smiled.

Scott grabbed his jacket, gave Ashley a hug and headed for the door. "I'll get the data to my friend so she can check it out. We'll touch bases in the morning."

"Hopefully we'll know more then."

After Scott left, Ashley made more copies of the drive. She hid one in her cottage and triple sealed one inside plastic bags that she buried in the yard.

She awoke the next morning from vivid dreams of being chased by faceless men in suits. She stopped at Java Joe's on the way to work for a mocha for Rob before driving to the *Times* where she found him in the PC Lab working on a server.

"Can you help me send more messages without them knowing it came from me?" she said, setting the mocha down beside him.

He looked up, blinking like an owl behind his glasses, smiling when he saw the mocha. "Can I help you spam messages without them knowing where it came from?" He rubbed his chin thoughtfully. "Let me see. Does a chicken have lips? Does a snake have hips? Does a porcupine piss on a flat rock? Does a bear shit in the woods? Is the pope Catholic? Is the sky blue? Are you breathing?"

Ashley swatted him lightly on the head and handed him the laptop.

Rob flipped up the screen and hit the power switch, keeping the banter going between sips of mocha, as if his manipulations were afterthoughts. "We'll show that spook Mossbarger who's who in the zoo." Screens flashed while his fingers danced from touchpad to keyboard. He popped disks in and out of the drive, typed and clicked, finishing with an icon in the top left corner of her screen.

"Take this to any coffee shop with wireless," Rob said, patting the display. "I'll have a bogus account set up on Gmail by the time you get there."

"Password?"

"IRSSUCKS."

CHAPTER EIGHT

The last rays of the setting sun shone through the tinted window on the west side of the *Times* building, bathing the newsroom's cubicles in late afternoon gold by the time Ashley made it back to her office. She felt nervous after sending Justin Stephens' letter to every email address she had.

Seeing lights on in her office, she steeled herself, expecting Mossbarger, but to her relief she found Scott, feet kicked up on her desk, the latest edition of the *Times* spread on his lap. "Nothing from the cops yet," he said over the top of the paper.

Ashley motioned with her head for Scott to come out of the office. "I'm still worried about bugs," she whispered, taking him by the arm and leading him across the newsroom. "Hear anything from your friends at San Diego State?"

"Tonight," he said, glancing up at the monitors. "They're anxious to talk."

"Anything from Jeff?"

"He called about twenty minutes ago jabbering about a meeting with one of his sources. No one can find any record of Stephens or Chris Daniels. No trace of Genengineering either."

"Why doesn't that surprise me?" She pulled him beneath the news monitors, feeling safer in the mix of television voices. "None of this adds up and nobody's got any proof of anything. It seems like the more we look, the less we find."

Scott stuck his hands in his pockets and scanned the room, then spoke in a half-whisper. "One of Jeff's contacts freelances for the CIA. He literally knows where bodies are buried." He checked the room again. "Let's get out of here. I feel like I'm on display." He pulled his keys from his pocket.

Forty-five minutes later they circled San Diego State's parking lot until they found a place to park, then they set out on foot for the Life Sciences building. After getting lost twice, they found Scott's friend and her partner in a lab full of flickering readouts, units with see through doors, hydraulic tubes, and racks of tiny glass vials. Charts, graphs, and computer screens showing yellow, green, red, and blue bands of DNA sequences filled the spaces not taken by instruments.

Two women looked up when Scott knocked on the door jamb. Both sported white lab coats, long dark hair tied back, and expressive hazel eyes that looked exaggerated behind matching glasses. Kari had a fuller face and Felise looked taller, but they could have been sisters.

Kari held out her hand. "Hi Scott," she said. "You must be Ashley."

"And I'm Felise," her partner said, coming up a side aisle. She nodded to Scott with a familiarity that said they had met before.

"Where did you get that crazy stuff you sent us?" Felise asked as they shook hands.

"Email."

"Either someone with a lot of knowledge about genetics is playing a big hoax," Felise said.

"Or it's the real thing," Kari finished. "The formulas appear to be valid, but without tangible proof…"

Felise picked up again. "If it is a hoax, someone with an extensive grasp of genetic theory went through a lot of trouble to make it plausible."

Kari waved for them to follow her to the back of the lab. "We're not saying it's true," she said. "We're saying his premise is solid and his formulas hold up."

"Do the pictures resemble anything authentic?" Ashley said.

Kari and Felise looked at each other, then Felise sat down in front of a computer with a large screen. "Chris's pictures are textbook examples of Progeria." She clicked the mouse through a series of screens until the haunted, emaciated image of Chris Daniels filled the MAC's twenty-one inch screen.

"An inverted insertion in the long arm of chromosome one in most of the cells." Kari looked Ashley in the eye. "The gene affected by

Progeria and Werner's are on chromosome number one."

Felise looked up from the screen. "What's been called the aging gene."

"Very specific and detailed information for someone to pull a hoax with," Kari added. "Textbook Progeria." She looked from Scott to Ashley. "But it's no sweat for some techie to doctor a photo, either."

"So you think it's a hoax," Scott said.

Felise pushed back from the computer. "Based on the evidence we've seen, we can't fault the math or the science of his claims."

"And we can't find anything that could disprove it either," Kari said, finishing. "Without tangible proof, there's no way to support or refute Stephen's claim."

CHAPTER NINE

Scott drove them back to the *Times* in silence, each of them processing what they had heard in their different ways. Ashley looked up as they passed the sign for Cox Arena. Talk about a cross between Frankenstein and Jekyll and Hyde, she thought. If Stephens is unstable like Mossbarger and Dawson claim, he's even scarier, because he's smart too. Smart enough to leave a puzzle that can't be proved or disproved without tangible evidence.

"I still don't believe any of it," Scott said, "but can you imagine what it would mean if he did discover it?"

Ashley couldn't think of anything to say.

When they reached the *Times* he turned his Accord into the lot and found a parking space under the building. They took the elevator up to the fourth floor where they found the activity in the late night newsroom subdued. Only a few people worked beneath the twenty-four hour news stations on the monitors lining the wall. Ashley's heartbeat quickened when she saw the lights on in her office. Shit. What now?

"I'll bet Jeff's been waiting awhile." Scott hustled to catch up. They hurried the last few steps, slowing when they rounded the corner to find Mossbarger slouched in Ashley's chair with his feet up on her desk.

Her breath caught. "What do you want?"

Mossbarger took his feet down and stood. "Thought you were funny sending email from a fake account, didn't you?"

"What are you talking about?" Ashley said, hoping her expression didn't betray her surprise. "How dare you come into my office and accuse me."

He jabbed his finger at her with narrowed eyes. "You won't think you're so smart when we find what's left of that kid in the bushes, sodomized with a broken neck!"

Scott stepped between them. "You got a warrant?"

Loud voices came from the newsroom before two burly younger men in suits came through the door with Rob Gubala between them.

"Have a seat," Mossbarger said.

"No thanks, I'll stand." Rob crossed his arms. "Hi Scott. Ash."

"Suit yourself." Mossbarger dropped into Ashley's chair. "We're going to be here awhile."

The two younger cops stationed themselves on either side of the door. Ashley shrugged and sat on the edge of her desk, thinking, where is Jeff Hamilton when you need him?

"We were just discussing Ashley's email stunt," Mossbarger said, pursing his lips.

"I'm glad you figured it out," Rob said, putting his hands in his pockets. "I was wondering how the son of a bitch was doing it."

Mossbarger leveled his gaze at Rob. His cop eyes looked expressionless.

"All of the problems we've had with our security." Rob threw his hands up and looked from Ashley to Scott, then back to Mossbarger, an exaggerated frown creasing his face. "Just last week some asshole got through our firewall and deleted Ashley's email account." He looked directly at Mossbarger. "That's the limp-dick piece of shit you guys caught, right?"

Mossbarger blinked.

Rob pulled up a chair, sat down and started again, eyes wide in mock amazement. "You haven't caught him?" He shook his head. "You mean to tell me that some little hacker is smarter than you Feds with all your super-duper snooper high-tech wowee James Bond…"

"You done?" Mossbarger cut in, looking so controlled it was clear Rob had struck a nerve.

Rob shrugged. "Don't be so hard on yourself. I understand how inadequate you must feel."

"Fraudulent Gmail accounts," Mossbarger said.

Rob looked out over his granny glasses at Mossbarger. "A pimply-faced script kiddy did all that and you guys *still* can't catch him?"

"Cut the shit, geek," Mossbarger deadpanned. "We know it was you."

Rob bowed his head, then stood, stepped closer, and leaned forward, smiling in Mossbarger's face. He hesitated for a beat, then said, "Prove it."

Mossbarger started to speak, stopped and started again. "It's only a matter of time."

"Well you're wasting mine." Rob started for the door, winking at Ashley as he passed. "I've had enough of your bullshit."

The cops by the door moved to block Rob's exit. He turned back to Mossbarger. "Am I under arrest?"

"No."

He started for the door again. "Unless you twerps want to get physical and get sued, I suggest you get the fuck out of my way."

They looked to Mossbarger with puzzled expressions. He waved them aside.

"I'll be in touch." Mossbarger started for the door, stopping beside Ashley. "Where's your shyster?"

"It's not our turn to watch him," Scott said, saving Ashley from having to answer. "It's late. If you don't have a warrant, you're wasting our time too."

"No, I don't have a warrant," Mossbarger said in a low voice. "I have a pedophile who's going off the deep end and a kid who will soon be dead and abused because a hack journalist doesn't want to cooperate." He slammed his hand down on the table, startling Ashley with his violence. "It's going to be on your conscience when we find the body."

Ashley withered under the rage in his eyes. A pang of fear touched her heart, making it hard to breathe when she realized that Mossbarger really believed Stephens was a murdering pedophile. Where was Jeff?

"I'm only doing my job," she said, feeling defensive. "I got that email from Stephens and I sent it out to some friends. There's no crime in that. If it was sent to me from one of your crazies, that's your problem, not mine. I had no way of knowing. I'm not trying to impede your investigation. I'm trying to get to the truth."

"Be careful what you ask for." Mossbarger's narrow gaze probed hers. "The truth might be more than you can handle."

"What's that supposed to mean?" Scott said.

Mossbarger held both hands up, speaking in a softer tone. "All I'm asking for is a little cooperation. Let us know if he sends you anything else, that's all. Work with us and I promise you'll get the exclusive."

Ashley looked to Scott. Nothing about this felt right.

"We'll be in touch if anything comes up," Scott said with finality.

"Yeah, right." Mossbarger shook his head, glaring at Ashley for an uneasy moment before leaving with his two men in tow.

CHAPTER TEN

S cott closed the door after Mossbarger, came back and took the seat behind Ashley's desk. His worried expression made her uncomfortable. "You're a good reporter, Ash. You know the importance of keeping an open mind." He looked straight at her, not saying anything for a moment, then, "You need to consider the possibility that Mossbarger could be right."

"Child molestation and murder?"

"Don't close your mind to it. That's all I'm saying. Stephens could be brilliant, but he's also human."

Jekyll and Hyde, Ashley thought, just like the story. "That's too big of a stretch for me. I just can't believe that a brilliant and dedicated researcher could be a murdering pedophile."

"Making someone immortal isn't any more plausible." Scott leaned forward. "I don't totally buy Mossbarger's story, but I'm not dismissing it either. Did you see the way he acted?"

Ashley sighed. "I have no doubt that he believes it. I can see it in his eyes."

Scott stood and went to the window, peering out at the newsroom. "I'm worried about Jeff," he said softly. "It's not like him to stay out of touch this long."

"Unless he's onto something."

Scott glanced at his watch. "I'm going to check my voice and email. Don't go anywhere. I'm sleeping at your place tonight."

"Scott…"

He shook his finger at her. "Don't waste your breath. I'm sticking to you until this thing reaches some kind of resolution." He put his hand on her shoulder, letting it linger for a moment before going out to the newsroom.

Ashley went back to her desk and saw the message light blinking on her phone. She pulled out a pad and pen and punched in her access code. The first message could have been a man or a woman, she couldn't tell.

"I tracked you down through the email string," the sexless voice said. "We have studied the pictures and read the text. We believe in Chris's immortality. We believe Chris is immortal because he is the second coming."

Great, Ashley thought, waiting for the beep of the second message. Some religious kook has my number.

The second beep came.

"Hi Ashley, Jeff. I don't have a clue about who this Stephens is, but people are scared." He lowered his voice to a half-whisper. "Even the spooks are spooked. I have a meet set up through a friend of a friend. I'll meet you tomorrow night at eight. Scott's office."

She heard a horn honking in the background.

"Gotta go," Jeff said. "Tomorrow night. Eight."

The line went dead.

She hung up, puzzling over the two calls. CIA spooks, religious fanatics, and a mad doctor. The whole thing sounded more and more like a bad B movie. If she had a nutty message in her voice mail, she dreaded what might be in her email. She turned to her computer and typed in her password. Twenty seven unread messages filled her screen. She did a quick scan, recognizing most of the names, except two.

One came from THE FIRST CYBERCHURCH OF THE SECOND COMING. It had to be the sexless weirdo from her voice mail. Her breath hitched when she read the second name. Chris Daniels. Knowing someone scrutinized her every move, Ashley double clicked the mail icon beside Chris's name. A letter filled the screen.

Dear Miss Butler,

I'm the one Dr. Stephens sent you pictures of. My name is Christine Daniels. In those pictures I look like a little old man, but I'm not. I'm a girl. Dr. Stephens was nice when he first helped me, but he's taking more drugs and he hardly sleeps anymore. I'm afraid he's going to do something bad. Help.

Christine Daniels

Ashley reread the letter, trying to get a better sense of it. Christine Daniels. A girl? What would Scott think? While puzzling over what to do, Ashley looked at the other email from THE FIRST CYBERCHURCH OF THE SECOND COMING. She smiled in spite of herself. This is the twenty first century, she thought. What will they say when they find out their Jesus is a girl? She double clicked, cringing at what was sure to come.

She wasn't disappointed.

The file had a blown up image of the younger looking pictures of Chris Daniels from the original email. Someone had changed the text beneath to read "Christ Daniels". The pictures looked more like a boy, but could pass for a girl. She leaned forward, rested her chin on her hand and read.

Dear Miss Butler,

Please put us in contact with Chris Daniels. I have evidence that his rebirth is the second coming of Jesus. This is a miraculous message from our Creator, calling us closer to one another.

Never before in history have so many minds been this closely linked. A man thinks a thought in Russia and moments later another contemplates it in New York. Because of the Internet, time and space are collapsing into consciousness. We who create, propagate, and populate this miracle of cooperation represent the universal mind of humanity. A noosphere.

Now the Power of creation has looked upon itself in man who is evolving toward a conscious group mind. Now that we are becoming one, Jesus has returned to lead us to new levels of being. Chris is the catalyst that will ignite this multitude of minds — of souls, fusing them into a unity that dissolves all boundaries.

The second coming has occurred at this point in our development as a natural blossoming of the divine plan for humanity. What better way for God to get our attention?

Please put us in contact with Chris Daniels. He is the light, the life, and the power. The glory of creation and the light of God shine through him.

Our website is under construction at:

WWW.CYBERCHRIST.ORG

Please forward this email to everyone you know. We need to find Chris to find Christ.

Sincerely,

Reverend Lisa Linton

Ashley closed the email and sat back, struggling to understand what was happening. This whole thing got crazier by the minute – as if each new player that weighed in upped the loony quotient. She heard it in her mind like some crazed game show host. "Top that delusion. See who wins the million dollar delusion." She was so lost in her thoughts she didn't hear Scott's approach.

"Hey, Ash," he said.

She jumped, putting her hand to her heart. "You scared the shit out of me." She sighed, trying to calm her pounding heart. "More email. One says Chris Daniels is a girl named Christine, the other says that Chris is the second coming of Christ."

His eyes grew wide, then, "Can you imagine the chaos that would break out if it was the second coming and Jesus came back as a woman?"

CHAPTER ELEVEN

Ashley shook her head. "I don't know what to believe anymore." She moved from behind her desk so Scott could sit. "Take a look. I'm sure Mossbarger's already seen everything."

Scott dropped into her chair and leaned toward the monitor. Ashley kept quiet, watching his changing expressions while he read. A puzzled look pinched his face when he closed the emails.

"This child abuse stuff gives me a bad feeling," he said. "Now we get a letter from the kid. A girl!"

Ashley motioned toward the door with her head. Scott nodded and logged off.

"I changed my mind," he said, once they were out in the newsroom. "I want you to stay at my place tonight. I'll sleep on the couch."

"I'm not going to put you out," Ashley said.

"It's not up for discussion." The tone in his voice said no argument.

"Can we at least stop by my place to get some things?"

"We'll take your car, then come back and get mine."

Ten minutes later, Ashley drove them west on I-8, heading down Ocean Beach Freeway. "How do you explain the cover–up stuff?" she said. "What about the Genengineering disappearance and that guy Holmstedt in La Jolla?"

"I'm hoping Jeff will know."

She hit the steering wheel. "I almost forgot. He left me a voice mail. Tomorrow night at eight. Your office."

Scott stretched his legs and put his hands behind his head. "If Stephens is a killer, I can see why the government wants to cover things up. A researcher who works with children and turns out to be a trap door spider is a public relations nightmare."

"I don't believe it."

"You don't believe it's the second coming either, do you?"

Ashley didn't answer.

Scott looked over at her, eyebrow raised.

"I'm not ruling anything out," she said after an awkward moment. She reached the end of the freeway and turned onto Sunset Cliffs Boulevard. "What do you think about that email from Christine?"

"We need hard information."

Ashley guided her car through the fifties style storefronts of Ocean Beach, zig-zagging down back streets to her cottage. She hurried inside, grabbed an overnight bag and stuffed it with clothes, toothbrush, makeup, and other necessities, then she drove them back to the *Times*. Moments after pulling into the lot, Scott drove back out in his car with Ashley slouched down below the dash. He pulled onto the freeway, periodically checking his rear view mirrors.

"See anybody?" Ashley said after awhile.

Scott motioned her up with his hand.

Ashley sat up and looked out at the lights of Mission Bay reflecting off the waters as they headed north toward Scott's condo in Del Mar. He took the Carmel Valley Road exit and drove along the salt water marshes toward the beach for a few minutes before pulling the car into the garage of his beach townhouse. Three messages waited on his answering machine. The first two were telemarketers. Jeff Hamilton's breathless voice crackled from a cell phone on the third.

"Hey Scott. I'm not saying shit about what I've found on the phone. Remember that bar we went to in Pacific Beach the night we were working on that skinhead story? Meet me there tomorrow at two. Make God-damned sure no one follows you."

CHAPTER TWELVE

The sour smell of perpetually spilled beer met Scott and Ashley at one forty-five the following afternoon at the doorway to The Pennant, a local surfer hang out in Pacific Beach. Stevie Ray Vaughan blasted *Crossfire* from the jukebox. Two bleach-haired young surfers played pool in the far corner and three barely of age girls in bikini tops sat at the four sided bar near the entrance. An older dishwater blonde woman with saggy braless breasts under a halter top nursed a long necked Budweiser while watching the pool game from the far corner.

Ashley took a booth by the window while Scott ordered a couple of Coronas at the bar where the three bikini top girls whispered amongst themselves. Scott smiled at them and whisked the Coronas away.

"Looks like you have a fan club," Ashley said when he slid into the booth with her.

Scott gave her a sheepish grin and checked his watch. "Jeff's due in ten minutes. He's always on time."

Ashley sipped her Corona, wondering how much more cloak and dagger she'd have to put up with. Scott had driven up and down Mission Boulevard, then in and out of single lane alleys, circling The Pennant for twenty minutes to make sure no one followed.

When two o'clock came, Ashley felt like jumping out of her seat. At two-fifteen, the beer in her stomach had shrunk into a hard ball and her underarms felt damp with sweat. By two-thirty, she felt as if she'd imploded. "Maybe we got our signals crossed," was all she could think of to say. The thought that something might have happened to Jeff was something she refused to accept.

"I could swear he meant two in the afternoon." Scott drained his beer. "Maybe he meant closing time."

Ashley's mind leaped on that. "I'm sure that's what he meant."

"Either that or he was being followed or something. I'm thinking he'll show up in my office tonight the way we originally planned."

They waited another half hour before driving back to the *Times*, hoping for a message from Jeff. Before going to their offices, Scott made Ashley promise she wouldn't go anywhere without him.

Back at her desk she found another email from the Reverend Lisa Linton of The First Cyberchurch of the Second Coming, trumpeting their website.

"Come on over to my office," Scott said, when she told him about it. "Let's check it out while we wait for Jeff. If he doesn't show up here, we'll check the bar again at closing time."

"What if he doesn't show?"

"Let's think positive."

"It isn't like him to drop out without a message of some kind."

"Unless he's laying very low. Come on, Ash. Email me that web address."

She sighed. "Okay."

After forwarding the message she went to Scott's office to wait for Jeff and see what the First Cyberchurch of the Second Coming had to offer in the way of online salvation.

Scott's corner windowed office looked out over Mission Valley. Poster sized color prints of him riding huge curling waves and a picture of a younger Scott with a group of surfers leaning against longboards filled one wall. Bright blue prints of every wave imaginable filled the other. The lights of early evening Mission Valley began winking to life on the other side of the full length tinted windows.

Scott looked up from his monitor when Ashley entered. "Pull up a chair," he said, waving her over.

Ashley dragged a chair around beside Scott in time to see The First Cyberchurch of the Second Coming's web page filling the screen.

"Jesus, they're serious," she muttered.

Scott let out a low whistle.

The supposed "latest" picture of Chris Daniels stared at them from the center of the screen. A bright white light glowed from behind Chris's head, giving a haloing effect that faded to sky blue before ending in an indigo tinge at the edge of the screen. The effect of the bright white set off against darkness made Chris's eyes look incredibly blue.

THE FIRST CYBERCHURCH OF THE SECOND COMING flashed across the top of the screen in alternating rainbow hues. A gold crucifix pulsed beneath it, above Chris's head. Below it, bigger than the rest of the icons, it said, **THE MIRACLE**.

Double clicking the icon displayed the sequence of Chris Daniels' transformation like the stations of the cross. A short caption beneath each picture proclaimed the blessings of divinity through technology.

Back at the home page, smaller icons lined the bottom and sides of the screen. A cross. Angel's wings. A halo. A dove. Under the cross it said, **THE TRUTH**. Under the dove, **THE POWER**. Under the halo, **THE GLORY**. Under The Angel's wings, it said join and become **ONE** with the **MIND OF GOD**.

Scott clicked on the wings and an email registration form popped up, complete with a check box for credit card donations and the promise of being assimilated into God's mind.

"They didn't waste any time getting their hand out," Ashley said.

Scott shook his head and clicked on the halo. A message popped up.

> Christ Daniels is the reincarnation of Jesus. His resurrection is the glory of God incarnate in man, risen up from the lamb. He has come to us because we have reached the highest level of self awareness ever known to humanity.
>
> Christ has come to lead us to the promised land. We must seek him in our hearts and in his presence on the web. He lives among us now. Flesh of our flesh. Bone of our bone.
>
> Help us find Christ so he may share his life and his teaching.
>
> Become one with HIM so the glory of GOD lives in us all.

Scott closed out **THE GLORY** and clicked on the dove. Immortality. Justin Stephen's explanation of DNA, telomerase, and his claim of discovering the aging gene near chromosome #1 covered the screen; verbatim from the email Ashley had sent out.

"What will they say if Chris is a girl?" she wondered aloud.

Scott settled back in his chair looking pensive. "What'll they say if Stephens is a psychopath?"

Ashley's stomach tightened at that. She leaned forward, closed out **THE POWER** and double clicked on the cross. **TRUTH**. Another message opened.

> The cross is the junction of time and space. The center of the universe. **GOD**. Where we live. The place where we become one with **HIM**. It represents life everlasting. God's gift to us through Christ, **HIS** only begotten Son. It is **HIS** reward to us for seeking with pure hearts.
>
> We have come together as one mind. One heart. One spirit. Through the miracle of creation, cooperation, and technology we have arrived at the meeting place of time and space. The mind of humanity.
>
> Our group mind is greater than the sum of its parts. It is the cross of humanity where we become One mind, One consciousness, achieved by working together through cyberspace; the foundation for **THE FIRST CYBERCHURCH OF THE SECOND COMING**.

Ashley leaned back and rubbed her eyes. She found the web page fascinating in spite of its bizarreness. Looking up at the wall clock, she saw that it was eight-forty five. The realization of time's passage gave her a sinking feeling in her stomach. Jeff wasn't going to make it.

He didn't make it to the bar at closing time either, so Scott drove to Jeff's house where they found an empty driveway and an empty house. After peering through all the darkened windows they drove back to Scott's in silence.

CHAPTER THIRTEEN

Ashley watched a pair of dark late model Lincolns pull into an excavated lot from her hiding place under the stairs of a construction trailer where Jeff had told her to wait. Two men in Hawaiian shirts, sunglasses, and floppy hats stepped out of the first car. Jeff and a stocky bald man climbed out of the second.

The first two smiled and waved. Jeff's partner nodded and stepped forward, Jeff following. After a series of handshakes, one of the Hawaiian shirts reached into the back seat of his car and pulled out a briefcase.

For no reason she could fathom, Ashley's heartbeat quickened when Jeff knelt beside his partner to open the case. No! She wanted to say, but the words wouldn't come. The two Hawaiian shirts took a step back.

The briefcase opened in a puff of smoke that sent Jeff and his partner toppling backward, clawing at their faces.

Silent screams tore through Ashley while Jeff and his friend writhed in the dirt, coughing and spewing pink foaming blood from their mouths and noses. One of the Hawaiian shirts slapped his partner on the shoulder and gestured in Ashley's direction, then the two ran toward her.

She willed herself to run away and scream, but nothing happened, further fueling her terror until she woke up howling and thrashing in a strange bed. She screamed louder when Scott burst through the door brandishing a baseball bat.

"Nightmare," she gasped.

Scott sighed and lowered the bat, taking a seat at the edge of the bed. "Scared the shit out of me."

"Sorry." She wiped tears from her cheeks. "It was about Jeff." She sobbed.

Scott slid closer and put his arms around her, gently pressing her head to his chest and stroking her hair the way her father used to.

"It's about time to get up anyway," he said after she grew quiet. He ruffled her hair, making her feel like a little girl. "I'll get some coffee going. You can shower first. We'll talk about it over coffee."

Ashley felt better after showering and the coffee helped, but her nightmare kept playing itself over and over in her mind. "He's gone," she whispered. "I know it."

"Don't give up hope," Scott said. "Don't *ever* give up hope."

"Let's check his house one more time, then we'll check in at the office." Scott put the paper down and sipped his coffee. "If there's no sign of Jeff, we'll put in a missing persons report."

"Okay." Ashley hurried to the bathroom to put on her makeup, then they finished their coffee and drove to Jeff's. Seeing nothing had changed, they headed for the *Times*.

"We'll check for word from Jeff first," Scott said when they pulled into the paper's underground lot. "If nothing's there, we'll get on the horn to the cops."

"I'm curious to see what's on my email," Ashley said, wondering about Reverend Linton and the email from Christine Daniels.

"The way this thing is breaking on the net," Scott said, hitting the button by the elevator, "we're going to have to put out a story whether Mossbarger's ready or not, otherwise someone else will scoop us."

They found no messages from Jeff at Scott's office, which didn't surprise Ashley. She knew in her gut that Jeff was gone, but she had to know for sure. Scott was right. Never give up hope.

Her stomach went sour when they found Mossbarger waiting in her office, sitting in her chair, arms crossed, scowling. He stood when they entered.

Shit, Ashley thought. What now?

Mossbarger kept silent until she reached her desk, then he pulled a piece of paper from his pocket and slammed it onto the desktop. "What the hell is this?"

His violence scared her. Scott eased her aside and picked up a printout of the email from Christine Daniels.

"It's an email," she said looking up from the paper, meeting his glare.

"And I suppose you don't know anything about it?" he snapped.

"Why should I?"

"It was sent to you." He pulled out a second sheet of paper and tossed it onto the desk. Ashley recognized the screen shot by the pictures and the web address across its top.

WWW.CYBERCHRIST.ORG

"What is wrong with you?" Mossbarger said, sounding like a father scolding his teenage daughter. "What are you going to tell these born again fools when the sodomized body of Christine Daniels turns up in the trash at the Miramar landfill?"

Ashley looked to Scott, who spoke up. "She didn't send those emails," he said.

God bless him, Ashley thought.

"They were sent to her," Mossbarger growled. "And she's been sending them all over the Internet."

"And you get copies of Asshole Cop Quarterly sent to you," Ashley said, regretting letting her temper slip. "Does that make you responsible for its publication?"

Mossbarger picked up the papers. "Don't you see?" He softened his voice, pleading now instead of reprimanding. He stared at the floor as he spoke. "A little girl's in trouble." He dropped back into her chair, put his head in his hands and rubbed his face. "We don't find Stephens soon, it's going to get bad for the kid. We need your help," he said quietly. "Help us save Christine. That's all I'm asking."

"I'll do anything I can to help," she said looking from Mossbarger to Scott and back again. "But you're the cop. It's your job to find her."

"I need to know if you hear even one peep from Stephens."

"I'll let you know right away," she said.

"And I want to know if that shyster of yours comes up with anything," he said, pointing at her.

Her heart stuttered, making her head swim like she had lost her balance.

"Of course," Scott said. "We'll let you know as soon as we hear anything."

Mossbarger eyed them both, then shrugged and left without saying more. Once he was out of sight, Ashley and Scott hurried downstairs to a pay phone in a restaurant across the street.

"Hello," Scott said after punching in the number to the San Diego Police Department. "I'd like to file a missing persons report."

CHAPTER FOURTEEN

After filing a missing person report on Jeff, Scott left to catch up on his work with strict orders for Ashley to stay in her office until he came back. She answered all her email and found herself in front of her terminal thinking that it had been too long since she'd written anything. Convinced that anything she wrote would be scrutinized, she took a deep breath and tried to think things through. Chris Daniels. Christine Daniels. As much as she wished she could believe Stephens, the likelihood of him being a pedophile was more plausible than a discovery of immortality.

She clicked on her browser and studied the Cyberchurch's website again, thinking that she knew what she had to do. This was one email Mossbarger would condone. She clicked on the link to Reverend Linton's email and began to type.

Dear Reverend Linton,

I don't know of any graceful way to say this, except that I have done a terrible wrong. The emails regarding Chris Daniels appear to be faked. It is a sad statement about humanity when someone stoops low enough to use a fatal disease to perpetrate a tasteless hoax, but it seems that the perpetrator is indeed a sick individual.

Soon after I forwarded his letters, the federal government made me aware of my error. According to them, Justin Stephens, the originator of the letter has deep seated psychological problems. I don't know what to believe, but at this point the government's claims are more believable than his.

I recently received another email from Chris Daniels. In many respects this last message is the most puzzling because in it Chris insists that HER name is Christine. Aside from the credibility gap of the first emails, this last poses an even bigger problem for your faith.

Jesus Christ was a man.

If I had any idea that things would go this far, I never would have forwarded those emails. Please accept my humblest apologies.

Sincerely,

Ashley Butler

Ashley hit the send button, feeling remorse over the loss of the hope of immortality she had destroyed in Lisa Linton and her church. She looked up from her screen and saw Scott coming toward her through the newsroom. "Come on," he said from the doorway. "Let's get some lunch."

He drove them to a sandwich shop on Prospect Street in La Jolla, then they took their lunch down to the cove where they ate watching the waves roll in, a favorite pastime of Scott's. The breeze, crashing surf, and the cries of gulls felt cleansing after all the things that had been weighing Ashley down. Jeff. Mossbarger. Stephens. Chris Daniels, whatever he or she was. The church. And she hadn't written a word in days…

"Cops say it could be weeks or months before we hear anything about Jeff," Scott said. "The longer we wait, the more likely…"

"That's comforting."

"And then those Cyberchurch people." He shook his head. "All the work that went into that website. I'm afraid to think of what a mess this could be if that kid ends up dead." His voice trailed off.

"If it makes you feel any better," Ashley said, "I wrote to Reverend Linton and told her that Chris is a girl and Jesus was a man, so it couldn't be the second coming."

"Something has to break soon." Scott checked his watch, stood and stretched. "Guess we'd better get moving." He drove them back to the paper where she found an angry voice mail waiting for her.

"Hello, Miss Butler," a strained female voice said. "This is the Reverend Linton from The First Cyberchurch of the Second Coming." The voice took on a self-righteous edge. "I'm sorry to have missed you, but I must tell you, it matters not whether Chris is male or female, for the Lord knows not gender. In fact, it would be more fitting for the Lord to return as a female in these troubled times. After being trampled underfoot for so many hundreds of years by males, the Goddess now rises ascendant at the beginning of this new age. Lest you write us off as another fanatical cult, I suggest you take a look at your email. Praise be to the power and the glory. Christ has risen."

Ashley hung up and hurried to log on. To her horror, a hundred and eighty three emails had come in since lunch, the first from Linton. She didn't recognize any of the others. The chime announcing new mail went off every few seconds. She snatched up the phone and punched in Rob's extension. He picked up on the third ring.

"I need your help," she said. "A bunch of kooks are flooding me with email. Can you stop it?"

"That explains why the gateway's been jammed."

"Can you stop it?"

"I'll put a filter on it that'll route most of it back to where it came from. Give me a few minutes."

She sighed when her incoming chime stopped a few minutes later. Two hundred and seven. They had been coming faster and faster. Most of the subject headings were religious in nature. Christ Is Risen. Glory to God in the highest. The Universe Is Oneness. Uni Verse –- One verse.

She deleted all of them except for eleven she recognized and one from Reverend Linton, which she read.

Dear Miss Butler,

I appreciate you writing me because I believe you think you are right, but I must take issue with your short-sightedness. I had a number of highly respected researchers study the claims made by Dr. Stephens.

None can refute it. Chris Daniels is the living incarnation of God. You say the federal government made you aware of your error and informed you that Justin Stephens has psychological problems.

This is blasphemy.

Of course the government doesn't want anybody to know. It's the same way they have kept their UFO contacts so secret. Unfortunately for them they cannot control the Internet. It is a medium for free speech, free ideas, and freedom of religion; a principle our country was founded on. Beyond that, it is the World Wide Web. A global community that no government can control.

It is also the collective consciousness of humanity manifesting in physical reality because of the minds that worked toward a common vision of communication that transcends the barriers of time and space. This miracle of Oneness has given us instantaneous transfer of thoughts, the same way they are conveyed in our minds.

Electronic bridges, hubs, routers, and fiber optics provide the synapses of this great mind. Trillions of miles of wire, satellites, transmitters, and receivers have been connected to share thoughts between us.

Technology is driving us and its evolution goes faster with each passing moment. It is the only industry in the history of the world where technology continues to come cheaper.

The Internet is humanity's global consciousness made physical. This is why Chris has appeared now. Mankind has reached a new peak, bending physical reality into a medium of thought that connects us all into the ONE that is GOD.

Mother Earth is Gaia. The Goddess. The nurturer. We are her children. She gives us life. If Chris Daniels is female, it is a fitting second coming for this new millennium.

Be still and listen, Ashley. Know in your heart that we are One. Join our burgeoning flock. I beseech you to help us find Christ Daniels, the second coming of Jesus incarnate in the global consciousness of humanity; the light and life everlasting. Praise be to the power and the glory for HE is risen.

Yours in Christ,

The Reverend Lisa Linton

Ashley bit her lower lip, disbelieving what Linton had written. Not only did the reverend not believe that the email was a hoax, she thought it was a government plot.

Ashley looked up when she heard footsteps and saw Scott pop his head inside her door. "What's this I hear about your email getting flooded by a bunch of whackos?"

She crossed her arms and nodded toward her screen. "Take a look."

Scott came around behind her and read Linton's letter with a growing frown. "Jesus Christ," he whispered.

"You'd better not let them hear you use his name in vain," Ashley said. "They take their blasphemy seriously."

CHAPTER FIFTEEN

It took most of the afternoon, but by day's end Rob had deleted Ashley's email account, created a new one with a different name, and sent her new address to those on her regular mailing list. Shortly after straightening out her emails, Scott called asking if she was ready to go home.

"Can we stop by my place on the way?" Ashley said. "I want to grab a few more things. Looks like I might be staying awhile."

"Let's do it."

Scott drove them to the end of the freeway and took the back streets, circling to Ashley's cottage in Ocean Beach to make sure no one followed.

"Come on in," she said, when he finally pulled up to her front door. "This might take a few minutes."

Scott hopped out of the car and followed her to the door. "Let's pick up some Thai food on the way home," he said. "I'm starving."

Ashley's breath hitched when she saw her front door cracked open. Heart thumping, she quickened her step, bracing herself for the worst. Scott pushed past her when she stopped in the doorway.

"Tossed" was all she could think. Cushions, drawers, files, and plants. Clothes strewn everywhere. Pictures torn from the walls, glass and frames smashed on the floor. She shuddered, thinking about what could have happened if she had been here.

Scott eased her back, put a finger to his lips and picked up a fist sized rock from her front yard before slipping inside her door. Ashley wanted to stop him, but felt too numb to move.

Who could have done this? Mossbarger? The CyberChrist church? Stephens? She peered inside where she saw Scott pull the phone from a pile in the middle of the floor. He looked up and waved her in. Ashley stepped through the mess, trying to avoid everything. She didn't know what she would have done without Scott.

He gave the police her address, then hung up and put his arm around her, walking her outside. "Let's wait out front. They said not to touch anything."

Ashley let herself be led away.

"This might be a little consolation," Scott said, "but your TV. and stereo are there. They threw your jewelry on the bed."

She nodded.

Two San Diego Police black and whites pulled up, double parking beside Scott's car. A tall sandy haired young cop hopped out of the first cruiser, approaching them with a purposeful gait, hand on his gun. A second, heavier older cop with a brush cut climbed out of the second.

"They're gone," Scott said. "They left a mess."

"Let's check it out." The two officers stepped past them and went inside, reappearing at the front door a few minutes later.

"They were looking for something," the older cop said, his eyes settling on Ashley. "Must have been scared off. Any idea what they'd be looking for?"

Ashley shrugged. With Jeff missing, she wasn't trusting anybody, police or not.

The cops looked at each other, then the older one spoke again, once more pinning Ashley with his eyes. "You ever been involved with drugs?"

She stiffened at his question. "Do you think I'd call you if I was involved with drugs?"

"They were looking for something," the younger cop said. "Most likely drugs. This is Ocean Beach, after all. Lot of freaks down here."

"Don't be ridiculous," Scott said, cutting him off. "She works for me." He pulled a business card from his pocket and handed it to the older cop. "Scott Miller, San Diego Times, City Editor," he said.

The cop studied Scott's business card before stuffing it in his pocket. "They didn't take anything of value, but they were looking for something."

A blue late model sedan with government plates pulled up behind the black and whites. The younger cop squared his shoulders and strutted toward the car. Mossbarger stepped out of it and started toward him, putting his I.D. in the younger cop's face saying, "Federal agent. This concerns national security."

The younger cop stared at Mossbarger's I.D., then Mossbarger pulled it back. "What's the problem here, Miller?" he said to Scott.

The older cop scowled. "Let me see that I.D."

Mossbarger handed it to him, giving his attention to Scott and Ashley as if no one else were there. "What happened?"

"Someone broke into Ashley's house," Scott said.

Mossbarger's eyes narrowed. "Anything missing?"

"Nothing that I can tell."

Mossbarger put his hand on Ashley's shoulder. "Come on. Let's go in."

"Where do you think you're going?" the older cop with the brush cut said.

"Where does it look like I'm going?" Mossbarger answered.

The cop looked down at Mossbarger's I.D. as if seeing it for the first time. "I'm running a check on you."

"Don't take too long. I'm a very busy man." Mossbarger followed Scott and Ashley into the house.

"How'd you find out about this so quickly?" Ashley said, feeling uncomfortable with Mossbarger in her house. She wondered if the flash drives were still there, but she wasn't going to look for them with him around.

"We picked the call up on our scanner." Mossbarger sized up her cottage, making her feel like her whole life lay open to him. "We were afraid of something like this," he said. "Stephens is beyond rationality at this point. Good thing you weren't here."

Ashley's stomach turned at the mention of Stephens.

"You think he did this?" Scott said.

"He's close to cracking." Mossbarger looked at the mess on her floor and held his hand out. "Who else would trash your place like this without taking anything? You can't stay here. I'm putting you in protective custody."

"Forget it," Scott said. "I'm watching her."

Amen to that, Ashley thought. "I can get along fine on my own, thank you."

"Only until we catch him." Mossbarger pulled out a cell phone.

"You're the only person he's contacted."

She crossed her arms. "Do you have any proof that he did this?"

Mossbarger finished punching in a number and shrugged. "Nothing's been stolen. It's him. I know it."

"We appreciate your offer, but we can take care of ourselves," Scott said.

Mossbarger nodded as he spoke into the phone, then his hand slipped inside his jacket, coming out a moment later with a gun. He ended his cell call, flipped the revolver open and spun the cylinder. Snapping it shut, he handed it to Scott. "Here, you might need this."

Scott held his hands up. "No thanks."

A knock on the door startled Ashley. Mossbarger stuck the gun back inside his jacket. "Hang on a sec, I'm sure San Diego's finest have cracked the case."

"Ashley, go pack your stuff," Scott said when Mossbarger went for the door. "We'll lock up the house and deal with this mess later."

"Okay." She stepped through the pile and went back to her bedroom to gather clothes from the floor. She stuffed them into a bag and grabbed her other necessities, then sorted through the pile on the floor of her closet checking for the flash drive she had hidden in her shoe. Mossbarger's voice startled her.

"You sure you won't take me up on my offer," he said from the doorway.

"Where's Scott?"

"Making a call."

She picked a blouse up from the floor and shook it out. "How do you know those CyberChrist people didn't break in?"

"I wouldn't worry about them." Mossbarger waved dismissively. "We checked them out. They're harmless." He pointed at her. "You're the one who's got them stirred up."

"I unstirred them this afternoon."

"What did you do?" he said, softening his tone.

"I emailed them after thinking about Christine's letter." She turned from him to finish packing a bag. "As uncomfortable as you make me feel, Scott's convinced me that the chances of Stephens being a psycho are more likely than his claim of discovering immortality."

Mossbarger's smile grew so big it looked unnatural. "That boss of yours is smarter than he looks."

"I told Reverend Linton that the email was a hoax and that the government showed up and told me Stephens had problems, then I told her about the email from Christine which proves them wrong about their second coming because Jesus was a man."

"You ready, Ash?" Scott called from the other room.

She glanced at Mossbarger, then started past him.

"Listen," he said, putting his hand on her shoulder. His touch felt creepy. "We want you back on line to help us catch him before he does some real damage."

"You mean bait?"

"You're the only one he's contacted." He lowered his voice. "You could save Christine's life."

"I'll give it some thought." She started past him again, but he held on.

"Don't take too much time. I'd hate to think of you living with Christine's death on your conscience."

"I told you I'd give it some thought." She brushed his hand from her shoulder and pushed past him to the other room. Scott took her bag and carried it out to the car.

"Why'd you get so pissed at him?" Scott said when they left Mossbarger standing in the street. "I think he's on the level about the Daniels kid. You can see it in his face."

"That's not the issue. There's something else. I'm surprised you haven't noticed."

"Noticed what?"

"Mossbarger's haunted us, what -- half a dozen times since we were first blessed with his presence?"

"And?"

"Other than a couple of times after this mess started, he's never once asked us where Jeff has been."

CHAPTER SIXTEEN

Ashley lay awake in Scott's bed listening to him snore from the couch in his living room. Now that she was alone she realized she'd rather have him closer, even if he did snore. At least then she wouldn't feel so jumpy.

Queasiness tickled her stomach when she thought about Jeff's disappearance. The questions and possibilities it raised sent her mind spiraling in too many directions. She pulled the covers closer to her chin. Mossbarger knew about her cottage being ransacked a little too quickly for her comfort. Why wouldn't he know about Jeff? It seemed like he knew about everything else. She considered asking him directly until his voice boomed through her mind as if to answer. "Be careful what you ask for, it might be more than you can handle."

She shivered at that. Could she handle it? Better still, did she have any choice? She rolled onto her stomach and buried her face in the pillow. Nowhere to go. Nowhere to turn. Nothing she could do except stay close to Scott and see what happened next. At this point it didn't matter if she agreed to help Mossbarger or not, they were already using her for bait, only they hadn't counted on hooking a hornet's nest like the Cyberchurch.

She rolled over onto her back and drifted for what seemed a few seconds before waking to full daylight and the local news on Scott's radio alarm. Feeling as if she hadn't slept, Ashley showered and put on her makeup, then went to the kitchen where she found a warm bran muffin and a cup of coffee waiting. Scott sat at the table drinking coffee while reading the paper.

"Thanks," Ashley said, settling into a chair. She sipped her coffee and peeled the paper off of her muffin.

Scott set the newspaper aside. "You going to help Mossbarger?"

Ashley shook her head. "Too many unknowns and not enough explanations. They're reading my email and listening to my conversations anyway. There's nothing else I can do."

"Good point." He drank the last of his coffee and stood. "I'll be ready in about twenty minutes."

They went to their separate offices at the *Times*, both promising not to leave without the other. Ashley felt a swell of gratitude for Rob when she found her computer configured with a new email address and her old address book. As quirky as he was, when it came time to deliver, he always came through. She emailed, thanking him, then started a letter to everyone else on her address list, telling them her account had crashed. When she finished, Ashley looked out at the newsroom, watching heads pop up and down from cubicles like targets in a crazy whack-a-mole game. The relentless clicking of keyboards reminded her that she hadn't written in days.

Clenching and unclenching her fingers, she felt the events of the past few weeks racing through her mind, ready to fly from her fingertips. Maybe she *should* be writing. If nothing else she could start a journal, but she had to make sure her work stayed on the laptop and she had to keep that in her sight — off the network.

Smiling to herself, she pulled the computer from its case, flipped up the screen and hit the on switch. While the system whirred to life, she felt a lead-in gelling in her mind. Who do you think you're kidding? She thought ruefully. This will be a far cry from a journal. Her fingers flew across the keyboard as soon as her word processor popped up.

A government cover-up appears to be occurring in San Diego County, centered around the death and disappearances of people tied to a business that has no record of its existence. The only person with any ties to this mystery sent out an email with the wild claim that he had discovered the secret of immortality. The government intercepted this same message and confiscated the computer it had been sent to.

The phone rang, startling her. Ashley took a deep breath and snatched it up. "Hello?"

"You going to be ready for lunch in a few minutes?" Scott asked.

"Yeah sure." She breathed again. "What time?"

"Twenty minutes."

She hung up and hammered at the keyboard again.

> The government claims that the author of the email is a murdering pedophile. Oddly enough there are no public records of this man Justin Stephens, who claims to be a genetic researcher. Whether he exists or not, Stephens has been linked with noted gerontologist and National Science Academy award winner, Dr. Russell Holmstedt, who was recently found dead of an apparent heart attack in his La Jolla home.

The more she typed, the faster her fingers moved. Publishing this could insure her safety. If something happened after it saw print, a lot of people would be asking a lot of questions.

She read back what she had written and glanced up, expecting to see Scott when she heard footsteps approaching. Mossbarger stormed toward her, red faced, his fists clenched at his sides.

CHAPTER SEVENTEEN

flurry of emotions fluttered through Ashley when she hit the save button, the most prominent being guilt. Mossbarger tossed a handful Aof eight by ten color glossies onto her desk, sending papers flying. The colors and contrasts of the pictures caught her eye.

Green. Light brown. Red smears. Meat, Ashley thought, then recognition hit her in the stomach, making her gag. A bloody body. Puncture marks. Eyes slashed. Arms and legs severed. Genitals and face. Mutilated.

"Christine Daniels," Mossbarger said, in a voice that sounded like it came from the end of a long tunnel.

Ashley looked from the picture to Mossbarger's angry face, frightened by the fire in his small dark eyes.

"We found her in a ditch alongside I-8 East of El Cajon."

Ashley could barely get the words out. "How do you know it's her?"

Mossbarger slammed a manila file down on her desk. "Fingerprints and dental records," he growled. "Stephens's hairs, saliva, and semen are all over her."

Ashley punched in Scott's extension with shaking fingers. Her hands and feet grew cold and her underarms felt wet. Scott picked up on the second ring.

"I need you right now," she managed. "Mossbarger's here with pictures. He says Stephens killed Christine Daniels."

"On my way."

Mossbarger jabbed at one of the pictures. "See those U-shaped wounds?" he said, sounding level and clinical. "Bite marks. He sodomized her too. Tore her sphincter…"

"That's enough," Ashley said, pushing the pictures away.

Mossbarger pushed them back. "Take a good look. If you had cooperated sooner we might have prevented this."

Scott hurried into the room. Mossbarger pointed to the mess on Ashley's desk. "Now that Stephens has popped the next one will come easier."

Ashley's anger took hold. "How can you be so sure?"

Mossbarger nodded toward the desk. "Four investigators in the FBI's criminal profiling unit have been working on this for the past two months. So far Stephens has done everything they said he'd do."

Ashley both saw and felt the pain that raged in Mossbarger's eyes. Her vision blurred from her tears.

"You need to get out of this fantasy world you've been living in," Mossbarger continued, looking from Ashley to Scott. "You're the only one who can help us." He tossed a business card onto her desk. "Every minute you waste is a minute closer to another death." He walked out leaving the photos and files scattered in front of her.

Feeling hot and prickly, Ashley drew in a long shaky breath and wiped the tears from her eyes. Scott's hand settled on her shoulder. "Don't listen to his bullshit," he said softly. "There's no way you're responsible for that kid's death."

Ashley stared at the desk full of pictures, unable to bring herself to touch them.

"I'll get rid of that crap." Scott stuffed the pictures and files into an envelope. Ashley held out her hand.

"You sure?" Scott said.

She nodded. As much as she hated it, she'd take another look when she felt stronger. She dropped the envelope into the bottom drawer of her desk. "Let's get out of here."

She set the laptop in its case and started for the door, then went back for the envelope. She didn't think she'd be coming back to work today.

They took Scott's car, heading west until they drove along Sunset Cliffs Boulevard with the windows down letting the ocean breeze blow over them. Scott found a turn off above the cliffs where seagulls and pelicans glided over the surf.

Ashley jumped out of the car and walked to the edge of the cliff, letting the smell of salt air fill her lungs while the plaintive cries of gulls and the roar of the surf filled her ears. The sun felt warm, but the steady breeze kept her cool.   What were the Cyberchurch people going to think now? She wondered. Chris Daniels -- Christine Daniels. Dead. Should she share the pictures? And Justin Stephens. Had he trashed her cottage? What if he tried to get her?

Tears streamed down her cheeks, cooled by the salt air. Come on, she told herself. Get it together. You can't sit around letting everything happen to you. You have to act. Do something! She turned to see Scott leaning back in the front seat of his car with his eyes closed. What did he think?

Scott opened his eyes when she started toward the car, watching her as she approached. She pulled open the passenger door and dropped into the seat beside him. "You think Stephens did it, don't you?"

He nodded.

"Okay," she said, folding her arms. "Take me to Mossbarger. Let's help him catch the son-of-a-bitch."

CHAPTER EIGHTEEN

The makeshift white cardboard sign above the door said:

FEDERAL TASK FORCE.

Mossbarger, the men he'd had with him at the *Times*, and the gawky kid who hijacked Ashley's computer all manned desks in a large office somewhere in the basement of a federal building in downtown San Diego. Ashley sat at a long table sipping tea while studying the pictures Mossbarger had tacked up on a bulletin board. He dropped a file in front of her. "Check these out," he said, pulling a chair up and sitting backward in it.

Ashley looked over and saw that Scott had fallen asleep with his head down on another desk. Sighing, she took the file and opened it. More reports and pictures of Justin Stephens. This was the information she needed to study the most, but her attention kept drifting back to the horror filled bulletin board. She sipped more tea, wiped her blurry eyes and looked up at the clock. Half past midnight. She and Scott had been here since six-thirty going over every detail of her connection to Stephens; everything except the whereabouts of Jeff Hamilton.

Ashley refrained from mentioning him, but as each hour passed, the question of his disappearance loomed heavier. She still felt suspicious of Mossbarger, but if the Feds had such an intense manhunt on for Stephens, they could look for Jeff too. To hell with it, she thought, pulling a picture of Jeff and Scott from her purse. "What about Jeff?" she said, handing it to Mossbarger.

He frowned. "Jeff?"

"Our lawyer. He's missing."

"Oh." Mossbarger handed the picture to the kid. "Check with the CHP, Harbor Patrol, Coast Guard, Border Patrol, Sheriff's, and San Diego PD. Have the FBI run a check too." He rose from his chair. "After the break in at your house, I've assigned one of my men to drive you home." He jabbed his thumb at Scott. "Two of them will be watching Miller's place."

Ashley scanned the file on Justin Stephens again. He looked like a big kid. Six foot three. Two hundred and thirty pounds. His short blond hair and cherubic, dimpled face suggested playfulness, but the twinkle in his blue eyes spoke of mischief.

She sorted through the rest of the documents. Born in Boston, Ph.D. in microbiology from MIT, interned at Scripps Institute in San Diego. A long list of research grants. How could someone so dedicated be so flawed? she wondered.

She looked through more documents before tossing the rest aside. "I'm not getting anywhere." She closed her eyes and put her head down in her arms.

"Reeth and Hart," Mossbarger said. "Take these two back up to North County so they can get some sleep."

"You got it, boss," the bigger of the two said.

Ashley stood, stretched, and shook Scott awake. He looked up blinking. "What's happening?"

"Let's go get some sleep."

Scott looked from Ashley to Reeth to Hart to Mossbarger.

"My men will drive you home," Mossbarger said, then to Ashley. "Tomorrow you can go back to work. We have taps on your computer and phone. Stephens will try to contact you again. No one knows we've found the body, so we expect him to keep trying to sell you his fountain of youth story."

Ashley felt too tired to discuss it further. "I need some sleep." She walked out with Scott behind her, followed by Reeth and Hart, who took separate cars, one in front, the other trailing.

Ashley dozed on the way to Del Mar, waking when they reached Scott's townhouse. Hart parked in front and Reeth took a spot on the far side of the street. Ashley followed Scott inside and went straight to bed, instantly falling asleep.

It seemed like a moment had barely passed when the ringing phone startled her out of a deep sleep. She sat up, heart racing, not knowing where she was. Washed out daylight from an overcast sky shone through the window. Eight in the morning by the digital clock on the nightstand. She heard Scott's voice from the other room.

"That's what I figured. No, that's all right. I'll tell her. We'll be in by ten."

He poked his head in the door a minute later. "I figured it woke you too," he muttered. "That was Mossbarger. They checked the morgue, the hospitals, the airlines, you name it. No sign of Jeff or his car."

CHAPTER NINETEEN

No more Jeff Ashley thought, eying agent Hart over the top of her computer screen. Gone. End of story. No one mentioned it and no one talked about it after Mossbarger's call. It felt like everybody went on with their lives as though Jeff had never existed. She knew to the core of her being that she would never see him again, just like she'd never see Russell Holmstedt, Chris Daniels, or anybody who ever worked at Genengineering.

Numb from the specter of Jeff's absence and the lack of closure that came with it, Ashley could only go through the motions of doing her job. Outside of that she felt like a bug in a jar.

Weeks dragged by in maddening sameness. Knowing someone watched every moment of her life made Ashley feel more trapped with each passing day. Every morning Scott drove her to work with Reeth, Hart, Mossbarger and others escorting them there and back.

Since changing her email address, the flood from Linton and the CyberChrist people stopped, but the website remained active. Ashley wondered what they would do when they heard Christine Daniels was dead. She wanted to do her own investigating, but with every aspect of her life under scrutiny it didn't seem possible. The dorky little geek who worked for Mossbarger joked that her office had more microphones than a recording studio.

Today she sat at her desk like every other day, unable to work on the article she had started for fear of having it seen by her keepers. Everywhere she turned she saw cops and now she had enough. She needed some breathing room. She watched Hart dozing in a chair by the door, his head dipping toward his chest like one of those bobbing water drinking birds. Soon his chin dropped and his eyes closed.

This is it, she thought, grabbing her laptop and purse. She took a deep breath and tip-toed past him. Once out in the newsroom, she hurried through the doors on its far side and made her way downstairs to the press room where she stepped into a small glass walled office to call Scott.

Three minutes later, he came through the double doors at the end of the press room. Ashley waved him over, then took his hand and led him past the rumbling printing press out to the loading docks.

A big truck at the end of the platform roared to life. Ashley ran for it, pulling Scott behind her. No sooner had he hopped into the back of the truck, when a bearded man in overalls pushed up the gate and pulled the canvas curtain shut. The truck jolted into motion a moment later, sending Scott flying into bundles of the evening edition. When they passed the front of the building they saw Mossbarger and Hart rush out the front doors. Ashley giggled and pulled Scott down behind a stack of papers.

"You're nuts, you know that?" he said, dropping beside her. "Christ, I'm too old for this shit."

"I need a break," she said. "We've been living in a fish bowl."

Scott sighed. "You're right. I was going a little nuts myself. What do you want to do?"

"Who knows where this truck's headed?" she said. "La Jolla, Del Mar, Cardiff. Wherever it brings us, we'll hop out and have an adventure."

"What if it's Barrio Logan, San Ysidro, or East San Diego?"

"Think positive."

They lapsed into silence as the truck picked up speed and rumbled down the freeway until it slowed and turned. Ashley crawled to the back and peered out from behind the canvas. You're not going to believe this," she said looking back over her shoulder.

"What?"

"Ocean Beach."

Scott crawled toward her, grabbed the lift gate and pulled himself up beside her. Rob Field passed by on their left and the Sea World tower loomed behind them. They hopped out when the truck stopped at the intersection of Sunset Cliffs Boulevard and Voltaire Street.

"Let's head for the beach," Ashley said, stepping to the sidewalk.

They followed Voltaire Street to the beach. Once they hit sand they took off their shoes and walked through the surf toward the Ocean Beach pier where seagulls and pelicans hovered over fishermen, and surfers caught waves. The roar of the surf felt refreshing.

"Let's head up Newport," Scott said when they closed in on the pier. They crossed a parking lot and walked up one side of Newport Ave. window shopping, then they made their way back down the other side of the street toward the beach. A man in bright tie-dyed pants and shirt hurried past them leaving the scent of patchouli in his wake.

"I'm having a flashback," Ashley said.

"You're not alone." Scott pointed to three women hurrying up the other side of the street, all wearing strings of beads and flowing peasant dresses.

"Something's up," Ashley said. "Too many hippies -- even for O.B."

More people came from a side street. Up ahead, they saw a crowd gathering on the grass to the right of the pier. Many carried pickets with someone's face on it. Ashley stopped when the shock of recognition hit her. "Son-of-a-bitch," she whispered. "Chris Daniels."

Beneath the picture she saw:

WWW.CYBERCHRIST.ORG

She smelled patchouli again. The hippie they had seen earlier handed her a flier with three pictures of Chris Daniels regressing in age. She read the text below it.

> Hebrews 11:6 "But without faith it is impossible to please him: for he that cometh to God must believe that he is, and that he is a rewarder of them that diligently seek him."
> HE is risen. Christ has come again.

The proof lies at WWW.CYBERCHRIST.ORG:
The First Cyberchurch of the Second Coming.

The squawk of feedback from a bullhorn grabbed their attention. A massive woman with long stringy brown hair dressed in a flowered smock stepped onto a platform. A huge gold Coptic cross dangled from her neck. Ashley knew without having to be told that it was the Reverend Lisa Linton.

"Christ has risen. Christ has been born again," Linton squawked into the bullhorn. She lowered it and scanned the crowd before putting it to her mouth again. "And the government is trying to hide it!" she bellowed, shaking a meaty fist.

A murmur ran through the crowd. Those passing out flyers moved quicker, spurred by her words. Picketers shook signs.

"A genetic experiment has been going on right under our noses here in San Diego," Linton crowed. "The result of it is the miracle of the reincarnation of Christ Jesus who has been made immortal through technology. The gift of eternal life has been granted to us by the Almighty and the United States government is trying to rob us of its glory. Let me hear you sing praise to the power…"

"Shut the fuck up, you wacky bitch!" Someone yelled.

Linton's eyes grew wide, then a bottle flew at her, knocking the megaphone from her hand. Pandemonium broke out as more rocks and bottles flew. Scott and Ashley ducked while picketers swung signs, fists flew, and sirens wailed. Four burly men in dark suits appeared out of nowhere.

Two grabbed Scott and two grabbed Ashley, shielding them as they dragged them off to a waiting car.

CHAPTER TWENTY

Mossbarger put his arm over the back of the seat and turned to Scott and Ashley. "Cute stunt," he said, matter-of-factly. "You're damned lucky you didn't get killed."

Ashley saw Hart glaring at her from the rear view mirror as he drove them up Newport Ave. toward Sunset Cliffs Boulevard. "You don't own me," she said, meeting his glare. "I'm not under arrest."

"How did you find us?" Scott asked.

"Never mind that." Mossbarger tossed a FedEx mailer into Ashley's lap. "This came while you were out screwing around."

Her breath hitched when she recognized the return address. 4458 Bird Rock Ave. She looked up and saw Hart's eyes still glaring from the mirror. Mossbarger turned toward her, his cold stare questioning. She saw Scott to her side, his eyes dancing somewhere between wonder and confusion. Shit, she thought. Nothing like privacy. She sighed and pulled the mailer open, finding a computer printed map of San Diego Bay with a note across the top.

Dear Miss Butler,

The government is lying. I never killed anybody in my life. I'm a doctor. A healer. If we can meet alone and in safety, I will share with you the most remarkable story you have ever heard.

Park your car at the Embarcadero at 5:00 tomorrow

afternoon. You'll find a blue and red skiff with an outboard motor tied to the pier beside the Star of India. Follow the route on the map. If I see anyone following you I will not show.

Sincerely,

Justin Stephens

Ashley looked first to Scott, then Mossbarger.

"What does he want?" Mossbarger said.

Ashley shook off a chill. "To meet." She handed him the note, thinking how Jeff must have gone to meet someone alone.

Mossbarger held the note up. "This is perfect."

"Do you see what he says about being followed?"

Mossbarger held up his hand. "We'll have enough surveillance gear and undercover men to cover any contingencies. Don't worry. You'll be safe."

"Why doesn't that give me the warm fuzzies?" Scott said.

No one responded.

Back at her office she found two younger, humorless cops stationed on each side of her door. She couldn't do anything without them seeing and hearing.

She picked up the phone and punched in Rob Gubala's extension. "I need your advice," she said softly. "Stephens wrote me a letter and wants to meet tomorrow. Mossbarger wants me to do it. He says he has surveillance gear and undercover people to watch me."

"I wouldn't trust those assholes," Rob said. "No matter what they tell you it's a lie."

"Can you find out how many links the CyberChrist website has to other sites? How many hits they get? How many people on their mailing list? Stuff like that."

"I'll get whatever I can."

"Thanks." She set the receiver down and saw her guards jump. Scott came through the door making calming gestures. "I'm her boss," he said. "I work here." He nodded to Ashley. "You ready to go?"

"Sure." She grabbed the laptop and the rest of her things. One of the doormen preceded them into the newsroom, speaking into a radio, giving location and destination. The second one took up the rear. The ride to Scott's condo in Del Mar didn't deviate from the procedure they had followed since Mossbarger started it.

CHAPTER TWENTY ONE

Ashley lay awake long past midnight, restless at the prospect of meeting Justin Stephens alone. The dream of Jeff's death looped continuously in her mind. The whole idea of meeting Stephens felt wrong. Too many loose ends. Too many questions unanswered. She couldn't trust anyone but Scott and Rob, but she had to involve them as little as possible. She couldn't live with herself if something happened to either one of them.

Drawing a long breath, she let it out slowly. She needed sleep. She hoped she would have enough time to get a feel for Stephens before Mossbarger and his storm troopers swooped in. That image made her thoughts come quicker and her whole body went cold and clammy. Holmstedt. Genengineering. Chris Daniels. Jeff Hamilton. Gone. She was about to meet the one person connected to all of them. If she disappeared there would be no one left to tell anything. Closing her eyes, she felt like she had just drifted to sleep when the alarm went off, jolting her awake.

After two cups of Scott's super-charged Kona coffee, a pair of plain clothes cops escorted them to the *Times*, once more taking residence inside her door.

She spent the morning writing her story on the laptop so no one could spy on what she wrote. The more she worked on it, the stronger her certainty grew that getting it published would insure her safety. If anything happened to her, a lot of people would be asking questions.

She read through what she'd written so far. A government cover-up, the disappearances of people tied to a business that itself had disappeared. A man and a boy with no record of their existence. Miracle emails. Confiscated computers. Internet religion.

She started typing again and was still going strong when the phone rang two pages later.

"Hey, Ashley," Scott said. "The riot made this morning's edition." Cradling the phone on her shoulder, she reached for the paper at the edge of her desk, flipped it open and spotted two columns under the title, RIOT RATTLES O.B.

"I'll call you right back," she said, finding the lead in.

> A riot broke out yesterday afternoon in Ocean Beach at a rally for the First Cyberchurch of the Second Coming, an online church whose website at www.CyberChrist.org sprang up as a result of an email hoax claiming the discovery of immortality. The Reverend Lisa Linton of the Cyberchurch claims the "immortal" young man she refers to as, "Christ Daniels" is the Second Coming of Jesus.
>
> The rally began peacefully until violence erupted between Cyberchurch members and a group of Fundamentalist Christians. Police moved quickly, breaking up the fighting before any serious injuries occurred. Reverend Linton and three of her followers were arrested and treated for minor injuries before being released.
>
> Since coming online, record numbers have "Logged on to Jesus" to become part of what Linton calls the linked mind of humanity. No other arrests were made.

Ashley punched in Rob's number. "Hi Rob, its Ashley," she said when he picked up. "What have you found out about the CyberChrist website?"

He let out a low whistle. "It already has hundreds of links. According to an independent survey, www.CyberChrist.org has the fastest growing volume of links ever seen on the net, and it's growing faster by the hour."

Her other line rang. "That's probably Scott," she said. "Gotta go. Let me know if you find out anything new." She punched the blinking line. "Ashley Butler."

"Mossbarger and a small army want to brief you," Scott said. She saved her file, shut down the laptop, put it in its case and slung it over her shoulder. "You bloodhounds ready to rock?" she said to her escorts.

The cop on the right nodded, then Scott stuck his head in the door. "Let's go see what Mossbarger wants."

Led and followed by escorts, Ashley walked with Scott to a conference room filled with over a dozen cops dressed as businessmen, homeless people, tourists, and gang members. Radios crackled and keyboards clicked. Maps, aerial photos, and drawings covered one whiteboard. The second looked like a football play diagram, with circles and arrows scribbled all over it.

Mossbarger looked up from a map, smiling expansively when they made eye contact. He was obviously in his element.

"You couldn't be any safer," he said. "We flew in our best undercover from all over the country. We'll be with you every step of the way."

He led her to two rows of monitors at the back of the room. Half had live video with aerial shots and close-ups. The other half, computer maps and three dimensional renditions of streets and buildings.

"You'll never be more than a few feet from any of us," Mossbarger said.

"What about when she gets on the boat?" Scott asked.

Mossbarger picked up a remote control and pointed it toward a monitor. An underwater scene flashed up on the screen. "The Navy loaned us one of their minisubs with high frequency sonar. Not even guppy shit can get near there without us knowing about it." He turned to Ashley and pulled out a heart shaped locket. "We got you this for good luck." He flipped open the locket, revealing a blinking green and red LED. "It's a combination microphone and homing device."

Ashley took the locket and put it around her neck.

"Meet us back here at two," Mossbarger said. "You're going to be famous as the woman who stopped a murdering pedophile."

"Why doesn't that sound reassuring?"

"You have nothing to worry about." Mossbarger draped his arm over her shoulder and walked her toward the door. "We'll have Stephens in custody before he gets within ten feet of you. I promise."

CHAPTER TWENTY TWO

Ashley followed Scott out of the conference room on shaky legs. Mossbarger's reassurances had the opposite effect and when he put his arm around her, his touch made her sick to her stomach.

"You okay?" Scott said, looking back at the guards following them.

She shrugged. "I want to get this over with."

He put his hand on her shoulder and gave it a squeeze, then checked his watch. "I'll be back for you in a couple of hours." He glanced back at the guards and turned down the hall toward his office.

Ashley stopped at the ladies room on the way back to her office, leaving her escorts outside. She saw no one in the stalls. She heard the click of a latch to her right and turned to see the broom closet door swing open. A big man in coveralls descended on her in silence. Short blond hair and a cherubic dimpled face. Mischievous blue eyes. Stephens.

She started to scream, cutting it short when his arm snaked around her neck. A cold metal edge pressed against her throat. Stephens' breath came hot and wet in her ear, sending a chill through her that rippled into nausea.

"One peep and you're a dead bitch," he said softly.

Ashley's knees buckled.

"Open your mouth."

Her jaw went slack and Stephens stuffed cloth into her mouth. She screamed in her mind when he covered her mouth and eyes with duct tape.

"We're going somewhere." He pressed cold metal to her ear. "You can't see and you can't talk. I'll have a gun to your head the whole time. You move, I pull the trigger. It's that simple. You understand?"

She nodded.

"Good."

He took her by the arm and swept her off her feet, catching her and lifting her into something big and round. He pushed her head forward, squeezing her knees into her stomach. She heard something being slid over the top and knew by the raunchy smells that he had stuffed her into a trash can. The thought of suffocation brought panic, but she couldn't move. Her heart thumped in her ears. She forced herself to breathe, gagging at the stink.

The trash can tilted back and moved forward smoothly. A hand cart. A muffled sounding door banged open and shut behind her as she rolled.

"Just finished emptying the trash before that babe came in," Stephens said. "So I bailed. You fellas have a nice day."

"Same to you," one of the cops said.

His pace quickened, making Ashley feel further from hope. They took an elevator down. Closer to Hell, Ashley thought. Vertical again. The top opened and a big hand grabbed her arm and yanked her up, then lowered her into a bigger square space.

The sound of a trunk lid slammed above her, followed by the click of a door latch. The roar of the car's engine preceded its forward motion, then they moved, stopping, starting, and turning. After awhile, the hum of the tires grew with their speed and they went without stopping. Freeway.

Engulfed in cold sweat and darkness, all Ashley could do was think, and the more she thought, the more she shook. Vivid images of Christine Daniels' mutilated body filled her mind while Mossbarger's voice boomed, "See those u-shaped wounds? Bite marks. He sodomized her too. Tore her sphincter…"

How long would she suffer? How much would it hurt?

Tears made pools beneath her blindfold while she shook with muffled sobs. Whatever Stephens was, the deaths and disappearances connected to him and the cloak and dagger stuff she'd been through in the last couple of weeks left her with one certainty.

She would soon be dead.

What frightened her more was what Stephens would do to her before that happened.

The hum of the tires diminished and the car slowed before going through more stops starts and turns until the crunch of gravel told her they had pulled off of the paved road. The car turned one last time and coasted to a stop soon after.

The engine died and the car door opened and shut, followed by footsteps. Ashley's heart pumped harder, but the steps receded, leaving her with nothing but the stuffy air of the car's trunk, sweat trickling down her armpits, and the clicks and tics of the car's cooling engine.

CHAPTER TWENTY THREE

Ashley stayed crunched in a fetal position in the darkness, desperately wanting to move. Her arms and legs felt cramped and her neck ached. She longed to breathe through her mouth again. Her heightened fear and the lack of stimulus that followed numbed her until she drifted into unconsciousness.

The sound of footsteps brought her awake. Her heart thumped faster, reaching its peak when a key slid into the trunk lock followed by the click and whoosh of its opening. Cool air hit her.

Night time, she thought.

Pain shot through her shoulder when a hand grabbed her by the elbow and pulled her up.

"On your feet," Stephens growled.

She stiffened and a slap stung the side of her face. "I'll gut you right here little sister. Quit fucking around and get up." Stephens pulled her from the trunk, half dragging her as she fought to stand on quivering legs. "C'mon, move." He pulled her by the elbow.

She stumbled along a hard surface until they reached some steps. Her knees buckled on the third one.

"Don't quit on me now, cupcake."

They went through a door, down a hall and through a second door where Stephens pushed, sending her sprawling backward onto a bed. "Don't move."

This isn't the way I'm meant to die, she thought, struggling to keep panic from eclipsing reason. Not like this. She listened to opening and closing doors, then felt his weight on the bed beside her. Hot breath whispered in her ear as he tied her hands to the bedposts. "I had a lot of fun with that little girl, but she didn't last very long." He grabbed Ashley's thigh and squeezed to the point of pain. "You should last longer."

This isn't happening, she thought, smelling the sweat of her fear mingling with the stink of the mattress. "We found her in a ditch alongside I-8 East of El Cajon," Mossbarger said in her mind. She envisioned his angry face and the fire in his small dark eyes. She curled into a ball until Stephen's hand snaked between her legs.

"No!" she screamed through cloth and tape. "No. God. Please no." Lightning stung the side of her face, rocking her head from a bone jarring slap. Stephens laughed and pulled her legs toward the foot of the bed. He tied her feet spread–eagled, then he put his hand to the side of her head, grabbed the edge of the tape and ripped it from her eyes.

Her skin burned and her vision blurred. Tears tickled the sides of her face, then wet warmth spread from her emptying bladder. They'll find me like this, she thought. Pissed pants. Men staring at me. Her eyes focused, bringing the image of Justin Stephens swimming into perspective, watching her from a wooden chair in the corner beside a darkened window. His cherubic face looked impassive, his blue eyes devoid of emotion. His mouth held a tiny smile.

"I really am a scientist," he said, "but I have an appetite that I can't satisfy." He rose and approached the bed again. Ashley drew a long shuddering breath through her nose. Her stomach churned. If she vomited now she'd choke.

Stephens stopped beside her. "Christine was too young. She couldn't appreciate the love of a man." He dropped onto the bed, grabbed Ashley's belt and loosened it. She squirmed at his touch until the tip of his finger pressed so hard on the end of her nose that her eyes watered. "Sit still!"

His hands moved over her and his moist breath oozed hot and sour on her face. He ripped the rest of the tape from her mouth and pulled the cloth from it. She barely caught a breath before he forced his tongue between her lips, making her gag.

Please let me die before he violates me, she pleaded silently. His hands moved to her breasts, squeezing and hurting. How she wished she could hurt him. Rage filled her and she struggled. Stephens laughed louder. To her horror she realized that her squirming excited him more.

He slid his hand over her stomach, undid the top button of her jeans and inched the zipper down. Ashley stiffened when he trailed the tip of a knife across her stomach.

No. Please don't cut me. Shhhh. Stay quiet. Lie still. Don't excite him. It will only hurt for a few minutes. Be brave. Muddled images of Chris Daniels played like a slide show in her mind's eye. Puncture marks. Eyes slashed, arms and legs severed, genitals and face mutilated. The cold knife blade slid up her inner thigh. She sucked air deep into her lungs.

Oh God please…

It moved up the other thigh.

Shhhhhhh. Stay quiet. Don't excite him. She closed her eyes, waiting for the inevitable. Stephens grabbed her jaw and turned her head to him. "Open your eyes," he whispered.

Summoning her strength, Ashley glared at him in defiance. I'm not dying like a coward, she thought in disgust.

He put the knife along the side of Ashley's nose and ran the blade down her neck, then he pushed her head back, letting the knife linger at her throat.

Do it now you bastard.

He unbuttoned her blouse. The knife moved down to her left breast, cold against her nipple.

"Ahhh," he groaned.

Bile rose from her stomach. Stephens pulled the knife away, leaving Ashley breathing deep, shuddering breaths.

"You're going to be a hell of a ride," Stephens said in a husky voice. He pulled his shirt up, kicked off his shoes, and had his pants halfway down his thighs when his head exploded in a shower of red that spattered Ashley with hot stickiness, then Stephens dropped like a punctured balloon.

She screamed her throat raw while doors slammed and footsteps came from everywhere. Two SWAT team cops in black uniforms and bulletproof vests burst into the room, guns pointed. Mossbarger came in close behind, gun drawn.

They lowered their guns when they saw what was left of Stephens twitching on the floor. Mossbarger came to Ashley's side, untying her arms and legs. More cops filled the room. Mossbarger pulled the covers from the bed and wrapped Ashley while the others huddled around Stephens. All she could see were his shaking feet. Mossbarger put a protective arm around her and hustled her out of the room.

"How did you find me?" she whispered.

"Your locket," he said, pointing. "Remember?"

"What took you so long?"

"We had to wait for a clean shot." He nodded toward the front door. "Pull the blanket tight. It's going to be a circus out there. I'll hurry you to a car and we'll get you out of here." She lowered her head while Mossbarger guided her out the door.

Colored lights flashed everywhere. Squad cars, motorcycles, and police vans littered the street. Yellow crime scene tape had been strung across caution signs. Uniformed cops held back a crowd. Scott came running up the steps, tears streaming from his haunted eyes. "You all right?" he said, pulling her to him.

She put her head on his shoulder, letting her own tears flow while he and Mossbarger led her to a car.

Halfway there she saw bright white lights bouncing toward her. "Shit," Mossbarger muttered. Her legs gave. Scott held her up.

A blur of red, yellow, and blue police car flashers painted the background while brighter whites punctuated the foreground, then the steady glare of halogens burned everything else away. Minicams and microphones closed in followed by a woman's voice. "What happened?"

Ashley's throat went dry. Thankfully, Mossbarger held up his hand, taking control. "Miss Butler risked her life to help catch a killer," he said. "She doesn't need any more stress. Back off and let us through." He waved them aside.

"Who's Miss Butler?" Ashley heard a reporter say as Scott and Mossbarger helped her into the car.

CHAPTER TWENTY FOUR

After a long, hot bath, followed by a shower to wash away the horror of her assailant's filth and her sense of being violated, Ashley had to sit through a battery of examinations, interviews, and a counseling session.

Following that series of ordeals, she ended up on Scott's couch staring at the television in a haze of Valium. Having no watchdogs made her feel both liberated and vulnerable. The jumble of images passing before her eyes looked and sounded meaningless and chaotic, while her experience with Stephens from kidnapping to rescue kept running through her head.

"It's eleven o'clock." Scott picked up the remote. "You want to see the news?"

She didn't, but she had to face it. Might as well take it head on while she was still numb. "Sure. Why not?"

Scott flipped through the channels until a commercial for Sea World cut to the opening credits for the late night news. No sooner had the credits passed when it came.

"In our lead story tonight," a baritone male announcer said, "An alleged killer was fatally shot by federal agents after kidnapping a San Diego Times reporter. Channel Eight's Laura Taylor was at the scene earlier tonight in South Bay."

Ashley groaned as a clip of her stumbling wide-eyed and dazed, wrapped in a blanket between Scott and Mossbarger played across the screen.

"According to sources close to the investigation," the woman's voice-over said, "Ashley Butler, a prize winning journalist for the San Diego Times had been working with federal agents on a hoax perpetrated on the Internet by the killer. Federal agents tracked the suspect to a Chula Vista address where a SWAT team sniper shot him in the head through a bedroom window."

Ashley clicked off the television, feeling stupid and victimized. "It feels like I've lost control of my life."

"Get out of town for a few days," Scott said.

She sighed. "I want my life back."

"What's it going to take?"

"I have to get to work on my story."

Scott held up a finger and went to his office, returning a moment later with the laptop. He held his hand out. "Stay here for as long as you want. Work as much as you want. But get some rest. You've been through hell."

"I appreciate you watching out for me," she said, meeting his eyes. "I'll take you up on your offer to stay. The last thing I want to be is alone right now, but I'm hoping that when I finish my story, I'll be ready to go back to my place. I'm beginning to forget what it looks like."

"Fair enough." Scott yawned. "I don't know about you, but I am beat to hell from all this. I can barely keep my eyes open. Let's get some shut eye. You can start your story after a good night's sleep. You'll be clearer."

The thought of losing herself in sleep sounded appealing. "Good plan. That's why you're the boss." Ashley stood and hugged Scott, then went to bed feeling like the last few weeks hadn't happened. She pulled the covers tighter to her chin while memories of her kidnapping punctuated by the horror of Stephen's exploding head filled her mind. She shuddered at the thought of what would have happened if Stephens hadn't been killed until something collapsed inside. She gave herself to the sobs that swept over her until she had no emotion left, and then she drifted into an uneasy sleep.

Scott's doorbell woke her. The blue digital readout on the clock beside the bed read 8:45. She closed her eyes, not wanting to leave the comfort of the bed, but the lead to her story kept pushing itself into her thoughts. After a quick shower she joined Scott in his kitchen where she found a postal mailer waiting for her.

"It's from Mossbarger," Scott said, looking up from his paper.

Ashley poured herself a cup of coffee, sat across from Scott and opened the mailer. It had a letter from Mossbarger and copies of reports from the Stephens case.

"What's it say?" Scott asked.

She unfolded the letter and read aloud. "Dear Ashley. Enclosed you will find pertinent details from my report of the Stephens investigation. Stephens was a government funded researcher, that much was true, but his breakdown and crimes were an embarrassment. I've taken the liberty of having one of our staff draft up a suitable story for you."

"Who the hell does he think he is?" She threw the letter down.

Scott stood and came around beside her, putting his hand on her arm. "Take it easy, Ash. Mossbarger is far from a charm school graduate, but he did save your life." He held up the newspaper he'd been reading. "Let it rest. You made the front page. You're a celebrity now."

Something sank inside her when she saw the picture of herself sandwiched between Mossbarger and Scott, her dazed expression frozen for eternity. "Shit."

"The picture's not so flattering," he said handing her the paper, "but the story is."

Tossing Mossbarger's letter aside, Ashley spread the paper in front of her and read the headline.

TIMES JOURNALIST HELPS
FEDS NAB KILLER

Award winning journalist Ashley Butler risked her life to help federal agents trap a murderer, who himself was fatally shot in a dramatic rescue last night in Chula Vista.

Butler cooperated with federal agents in an attempt to trap Justin Stephens, a drug addicted doctor who had kidnapped her hours before a scheduled meet. Minutes earlier, Butler had been briefed by government agents and amazingly enough, had just been outfitted with a homing device. Federal agents tracked her to a Chula Vista residence where a federal sharpshooter shot Stephens through the head.

"America doesn't have many heroes anymore," said Special Agent Mossbarger who headed the federal task force. "I've seen combat in Nam, been through shoot outs and hostage situations, and I can't ever recall seeing anyone as brave as Ashley Butler. Our country owes her thanks."

Mossbarger further stated that Butler's work helped culminate a three month manhunt that brought the task force to San Diego.

See Manhunt, pg. 3

"What a load of shit," Ashley muttered.

"Sounded pretty flattering to me," Scott said.

She flipped to page three and scanned the rest of the story. Detail upon detail of Justin Stephens and his aberrations, how he murdered, his pedophilia, psychiatric evaluations, interviews; everything about his psychological makeup.

No mention of Christine Daniels, Jeff Hamilton's disappearance, Holmstedt's death, Genengineering, Lisa Linton, or The First Cyberchurch of the Second Coming. Good, she thought. That's *my* story. She dropped the paper, picked up the mailer and pulled out the rest of its contents. The "story" Mossbarger's staff had written was identical to the one she had just read in the morning's paper.

"It's the same story they put in the paper," Ashley said, handing the mailer and its contents to Scott.

Scott looked from the letter to the paper and shrugged. "Looks like they're distancing themselves from the fact that Stephens worked for them."

"Not to mention the church, missing people, missing companies, and dead scientists."

"He's keeping that out for a reason, Ashley. Who knows what Stephens really did for them? He could have been a CIA contract killer gone off the deep end for all we know."

"What about his immortality claim?"

"The ravings of a drug addict who pushed himself over the limit," Scott said. "Christ, Ashley, this nutcase kidnapped you and was ready to slice you to ribbons. If it wasn't for Mossbarger, we wouldn't be sitting here having this conversation."

"You're right," she said, feeling shamed by Scott's admonition.

"I know you're going to write what you have to write. Think about it first, that's all. Mossbarger has good reasons for keeping that information out of the paper."

Scott's words spiked her anger. "I'll think it through before I write the story," she said quietly. Then I'll write the truth, she thought.

Scott studied her for a long questioning moment, then surprised her, saying, "Whatever you decide, I'll back you on it."

CHAPTER TWENTY FIVE

Ashley sat alone at the table wondering how she could feel angry at the man who had saved her? A shiver passed through her at the thought of what Stephens would have done if Mossbarger's sharpshooter hadn't acted. Yes, Mossbarger saved her life, but it didn't change the way she felt. Mr. SWAT Team had confiscated her computer. Worse than that, he had taken her words. Her First Amendment right. Same thing he was trying to do now. Her rising anger flushed the guilt from her and her heart beat harder. Jeff Hamilton had been silenced trying to protect her right. If she owed anybody, she owed him.

She reread the paper and Mossbarger's letter, thinking Jeff would want the truth, the whole truth, and nothing but the truth. That's the way it had to be. If she raised questions now, the limelight would protect her.

She pulled the laptop from its case and set it up on Scott's table. After it whirred to life she pulled up the story she'd been working on before all hell had broken loose. Flexing her hands, she put them to the keys, letting her thoughts flow and her fingers dance.

> The death of Justin Stephens is more than the demise of a complex and twisted individual. It is also the culmination of the equally complex and twisted circumstances surrounding his life.
>
> The tragedy began with an email Stephens sent to

this paper claiming that he had discovered immortality. The government intercepted the email and confiscated the computer it had been sent to, but not before the email was forwarded to others.

Stephens, who claimed to be a genetic researcher, had sent text and pictures of a child with an aging disorder named Chris Daniels, who according to Stephens was aging in reverse as a result of his discovery. Stephens claimed to have turned off the aging gene, making its carrier immortal.
The government said he was a murdering pedophile.

Oddly enough there is no public record of Dr. Stephens, who was linked to noted gerontologist and National Science Academy award winner, Dr. Russell Holmstedt, a man recently found dead of an apparent heart attack in his La Jolla home.

Local geneticists could neither confirm nor deny Stephens' claims based on the proof he had emailed. They did say that his theory and its supporting formulas were plausible based on what they saw.

Justin Stephens did work for the United States government. That much has been confirmed. What cannot be confirmed is the death and disappearances of people tied to a Sorrento Valley research facility that itself has vanished. Equally puzzling is the formation of an Internet church calling itself The First Cyberchurch of the Second Coming, which came into existence as a result of the Stephens email, which had been reposted all over the Internet.

The church's address at www.CyberChrist.org has the distinction of being history's fastest growing website.

Cyberchurch members believe that Stephen's latest victim, a child named Christine Daniels, was the living incarnation of Jesus Christ. The Cyberchurch's spokesperson, the Reverend Lisa Linton, believes that the federal government is covering up the discovery of immortality and that "Christ Daniels" is the second coming of Jesus made manifest online. In Linton's words, the World Wide Web "is the collective consciousness of humanity made into a physical reality because of the minds that worked toward the common vision of communicating with one another. It is our group consciousness made physical."

Who were Justin Stephens and Chris Daniels? Why is there no record of Stephens or Chris Daniels, who was first thought to be a boy, then later a girl? Has a divine incarnation once more found death at the hands of humanity? Has the secret of eternal life slipped from our grasp, or has our government saved us from a murdering pedophilic research scientist?

Ashley put her hands behind her head and stretched, sensing that she had captured most of what she wanted. She hit the save button, powered down the laptop, and closed it. After lunch she would give it a few more edits before sending it to the paper for tomorrow's edition. If nothing else, it would get people asking the right questions. Mossbarger would go through the ceiling when he read it, but that was too bad. She had played ball his way and almost lost her life for helping.

Scott came out from his office, poured a cup of coffee and sat at the table with her. "I heard you banging away on the keys so I left you alone."

She patted the laptop. "First draft."

Scott nodded toward the computer. "May I?"

Ashley flipped up the screen, hit the on button, and turned the computer so the screen faced Scott, then she busied herself putting water on for tea while stealing glances at Scott to see his reactions. When he finished reading, he looked up and shook his head.

"What?" Ashley said.

"Far be it from me to stop you from saying your piece, in fact it's my job to help you do that, but all this X-file government stuff scares the hell out of me, especially after Jeff…"

Her throat tightened at his words. "I've already been through hell, Scott. I can't sleep nights and I don't feel safe. I don't know who to trust and who to believe. I'm never going to be able to go into a ladies room alone for the rest of my life." She felt herself shaking. "I'm lucky to be alive right now. I've been dragged into some twisted shadow world of half truths. Everyone else who's been there hasn't come back.

Jeff, Stephens, Chris Daniels, Holmstedt. I'm the only one left. I can't help thinking that it's only a matter of time. I might be a victim of a drunk driver. A suicide. Drug overdose. Self-inflicted gunshot wound to the head. Most likely I'll just vanish."

"It's not going to happen," he said. I won't let it. I'm not letting you out of my sight. Not even to go to the little girl's room."

"My life depends on that story seeing print. The more people who read it, the better my chances are. I'll never be able to live with myself if I don't do the right thing. That's what Jeff died for. Getting this story out is the right thing."

She finished her final edit late that afternoon. Scott logged on from his home computer and submitted her story, following it up by calling the *Times* and giving orders to put it on page one. Ashley listened, thinking that in a matter of hours, her story would end up in stores, newspaper machines, and houses all over the city. What would come next?

They ordered Chinese food for dinner and watched movies on cable. Ashley felt relieved when she saw no mention of her adventure on the late news. After the news, they both went to bed.

CHAPTER TWENTY SIX

"Son-of-a-bitch!"

Ashley opened her eyes to Scott's angry voice in the gray light of morning.

"What's the matter?" she called out.

"You're not going to believe this." He came through the door, tossing the paper on the bed. "They didn't print it!"

Ashley's heartbeat quickened. "I heard you tell them. Wouldn't they have called if they weren't going to put it in?"

Scott looked at the clock and rubbed his chin. "Quarter after seven. Composing doesn't get in until eight. Damn!" He stormed out of the room. A sinking feeling settled in the pit of Ashley's stomach. Pulling on jeans and a sweater, she went out to the kitchen where Scott punched a number into the phone.

"Miller here. What happened to Butler's story?" A pause, then. "Are you shitting me? No, we'll be there in an hour." He hung up, a troubled expression pinching his face.

"What?"

"The publisher pulled it," he said.

"Why?"

"That's what we're going to find out. Relling would rather be drawn and quartered before pulling a story, especially one like this."

Twenty minutes later they drove south on I-5 heading for the *Times* where Scott parked in the underground lot. They took the elevator up to Relling's office. His receptionist stood and opened her mouth when they entered. Scott waved her off and strode past her, straight into

Relling's office. Ashley followed.

Bill Relling looked up through wire-rimmed glasses. His thinning brown hair looked mussed, like he had suddenly woken from a nightmare. His rumpled brown suit looked too big and his shoulders slumped as if he'd been beaten. "Something I can do for you, Miller?" he said.

"What happened to my story?" Ashley said, before Scott could speak.

Relling looked at her as if not seeing her. "My mother made me pull it. Said we had to help the government." He spoke faster. "They didn't want a panic and there was information they didn't want publicized. They asked you not to publish it," he said as if seeing Ashley for the first time.

"You're the publisher," Scott said, then louder, "You're supposed to print the news, not censor it!"

"My mother is the majority stockholder," Relling said. "She's the one who says what will be printed." His tone softened. "They're threatening us with an investigation. The IRS has already frozen our assets."

"So you caved," Ashley said.

"I'm doing what I'm told," Relling said, sounding like a scolded child.

"Well I'm not."

Relling's eyes grew wide behind his wire rims. "You will if you want to keep your job."

Ashley couldn't believe what she was hearing. "You're threatening me for doing my job? I'll be talking to the labor board faster than you can say civil lawsuit."

"Your job is to do what you're told," Relling said, jabbing his finger at her. "If you're smart, you'll forget about this shit and get back to work. Rumor has it there's a big raise in the works and a bonus. You're a star, Ashley. Don't blow it. I'm sorry your story can't be printed, but we've already lost a lawyer. We don't want to lose you."

She felt herself weaken. "It has to see print." She glanced at Scott who stared at Relling. "It's my only hope."

"Don't you get it?" Relling leaned forward. "Keep your mouth shut, you get a raise, a bonus, and some choice assignments. Do I have to make it any clearer?"

"If I refuse?"

"You're in the unemployment line." He pointed to Scott. "You too Miller."

Scott crossed his arms. "Whatever Ashley does, I'm backing her."

"Miller's livelihood is in your hands Ashley," Relling said, leaning back in his chair.

Ashley's emotions bubbled. She hated being pressured. Damn him, she thought. "I'll think about it." She caught Scott's eye and motioned with her head for them to go.

"Leave the laptop," Relling said.

"What?"

"You heard me. Leave the laptop. He pointed at his desk top.

"My story's on here."

"That computer is the property of the San Diego Times." He grabbed the phone. "Don't make me call security."

Ashley didn't move until Relling punched the keys on his phone, then she tossed the notebook onto his desk and walked out.

CHAPTER TWENTY SEVEN

Ashley followed Scott out, slamming the door to Relling's office behind her. She shook with rage, sensing the fear that simmered beneath it. "I have to find Rob," she said, hitting the down button on the elevator. "I need another laptop."

The elevator took them to the bottom floor where they hurried through the maze of corridors that led to the tech support lab. Ashley's breath hitched when she saw the lights out.

Scott flipped the switch, revealing a room full of flashing LED's and screen savers dancing across monitors. The message light blinked on Rob's phone. A three dimensional Star Trek screen saver moved across his monitor. Scott tapped the mouse and Rob's log on screen popped up. A cup of coffee sat on the edge of the desk. Ashley put her hand on it. Still warm.

"We'll wait." Scott dropped into Rob's chair and kicked his feet up. Ashley perched on a lab stool.

"Rob never shuts the lights off," she said.

Scott picked up the phone and called Rob, then started calling others. No one had seen him since yesterday.

Come on, Ashley thought, feeling more alarmed with each passing moment. Answer your phone, damn it. She flashed on her dream of Jeff's death and fought panic. Rob was gone. Her stomach knotted. "Come on," she said.

Scott came from behind Rob's desk and followed her out of the lab. Ashley felt better when they left the building, but she felt chilled under the weight of Rob's disappearance. Cold sweat trickled down the small of her back by the time they reached the parking lot. She scanned it for signs of Mossbarger's men before they ran to the car and pulled into the street. Seeing nothing out of the ordinary, she pulled a pad and pen from her purse and wrote.

DON'T TALK ABOUT ANYTHING.

Scott frowned.

CAR COULD BE BUGGED, she scribbled.

"Where do you want to go?"

"Sunset Cliffs."

Scott flipped on the radio and they drove west on I-8 to Sunset Cliffs Boulevard. Neither of them spoke until he found a view point clear of other cars.

"I need a computer and an email account," Ashley said as soon as they were clear of the car. "And all that stuff Rob gets me." They walked to the edge of the cliff. The salt air, surf, and its white noise washed through Ashley with the knowledge that she could speak freely.

"There's no place to go," she said. "No one I can think of to go to for help."

"How about one of those cybercafés?" Scott said. "You get a cappuccino, slap down a few bucks and they hook you up with a browser and an Internet connection."

"We need to email as many as fast as we can. Once they track down the source, they'll come after us."

"Come on." She took him by the arm. "We have work to do. We need to stop at my house first."

Scott drove them back on Sunset Cliffs Boulevard to Ashley's cottage in Ocean Beach, parking one street over from hers. She cut through a neighbor's yard, hopped the fence and retrieved the flash drive she'd hidden in her back yard. As far as she could tell, no one saw her. They drove north to a cybercafé off of Prospect Street in La Jolla. Scott circled the block four times before parking. No one followed them, which had the strange effect of heightening her fear.

Scott parked a block away and they split up, walking down both sides of the street, entering the café separately. Ashley went in last, finding the aroma of fresh coffee a little comforting. Computers lined the walls and filled a small cube farm in the center of the floor. Less than half of the booths were occupied. A long haired college kid with a goatee and diamond earring, wearing a U.C.S.D. sweatshirt looked up from the cash register.

"We'd like to rent some computer time," Ashley said. "And a latté."

"Make that two." Scott pulled some cash from his pocket.

The kid took a twenty from Scott and handed him some change. "Four and five over there." He pointed to the wall. "I'll bring the drinks to you."

"Thanks." Scott dropped a dollar into the tip jar.

They sat at neighboring terminals. Ashley copied her story from the disk she had retrieved from her yard and edited it all into one file that held pictures, graphics, emails, her writing, and everything else connected to the Justin Stephens mystery, including what she had on the Cyberchurch. Using a fake Hotmail account, she typed out a letter.

> Please read the enclosed file and then forward it to everyone you trust. Many people have disappeared as a result of this information. Each person that reads this increases the chances of my survival.

She emailed everything, first to Lisa Linton, then to everyone else she could think of. When they finished, they went back to Scott's feeling uneasy about the fact that no cops waited or came for them.

CHAPTER TWENTY EIGHT

Ashley spent another night at Scott's drifting in and out of sleep, wondering when Mossbarger and his cop army would come crashing through the door. After what seemed an eternity, she opened her eyes to the gray of dawn. Why hadn't the Feds come? They had to have seen her email by now. She smiled, thinking how Mossbarger must have blown a gasket, but it worried her that he hadn't come.

Outside the day grew brighter. When she heard Scott rattling around in the kitchen, she rolled out of bed and threw on a robe.

"How'd you sleep?" he said over his shoulder as he made coffee.

She sighed. "Like I haven't. Mossbarger should have come by now. I don't understand. What are we going to do?"

Scott poured water into the coffeemaker. "Go to work."

"After what we did?"

"You didn't publish the story and there's no law against emailing."

"What about Rob?" she said, feeling a tremor in her voice.

"Don't count him out yet," Scott said. "If there were government hit men on the prowl, they would have come for us by now, don't you think?"

Ashley wished she felt as confident as Scott sounded.

"And if we don't show up we'll look guilty," he added.

After coffee and a shower, Ashley dressed, put on her makeup, and hurried back to the kitchen where she found Scott muttering to himself while reading the morning paper.

"What now?" She said.

He slid the paper over to her, sat back and crossed his arms while she read.

CULT PERPETRATES INTERNET HOAX

By

Ashley Butler

A modern day version of a hoax reminiscent of the War of The Worlds radio prank performed by Orson Welles in the mid-twentieth century has been committed on the Internet by a cult calling themselves The First Cyberchurch of the Second Coming. The church has overtones of the Heaven's Gate cult that stunned San Diego with a tragic mass suicide back in nineteen ninety seven and is presently under investigation by numerous federal agencies.

The Cyberchurch, which staged a violent rally in Ocean Beach last week, has also been linked to Justin Stephens, a rapist murderer that federal authorities fatally shot in a dramatic rescue in Chula Vista. Anonymous sources claim the "Cyberchurch" is the originator of a fictional email sent out to the Internet by Stephens.

As a result of the scam, Cyberchurch members were led to believe that Stephen's last victim, a murdered child they had named "Christ Daniels" was the second coming of Jesus.

(See Cyberchurch – page A3)

Ashley threw the paper down. "Not only did they kill my story, they published this tripe and put my name on it." She grabbed her purse and stood. Her whole body shook. "I'm not going to let them get away with this."

"I have a bad feeling," Scott said, still sitting. "They put your name on a story you didn't write and discredited the one you did. You think they're going to let you march in there and tell them what to do?"

She put her hands on her hips. "Are you driving me to work or am I calling a cab?"

Scott stared at her, his face expressionless, then his shoulders dropped. "Okay."

Ashley wished he hadn't agreed so quickly, but Scott was in motion, so she snatched her jacket from the chair and followed him, gaining strength from his actions.

She stared out at the ocean in silence as they headed south, passing the housing developments and high-tech office buildings of Del Mar as they drove to the *Times*. Where the hell was this craziness going now? Lies, emails, taps, and online spying. People disappearing. She squeezed her hand into a fist. And the whole time the bastards shit on her First Amendment rights. She closed her eyes, not opening them until Scott turned the corner, bringing the *Times* building into sight.

She saw fluttering paper first, then recognized it as pickets. Had the press operators gone on strike again? Her breath caught when she recognized the man in the tie-dyed pants and shirt from the riot in O.B. He carried a picket that said: **HAVE YOU SEEN ME?**, in big letters with a life-sized picture of Chris Daniels. Women wearing strings of beads and flowing peasant dresses waved more signs.

STOP GOVERNMENT CONSPIRACY, one said. **THE GOVERNMENT IS THE TOOL OF THE ANTICHRIST**, another said. **SAVE WWW.CYBERCHRIST.COM,** said a third.

Faces turned toward them when Scott eased the car through the crowd. Ashley saw fliers everywhere with pictures of Chris Daniels that said, **HAVE YOU SEEN ME?,** in bold print.

"That's the hack who wrote all the lies," a voice said from somewhere. People moved closer, pressing their faces to the car's window.

"Satan's Tool," A bearded man with long frizzy hair howled.

"I'll give you Satan's Tool." Scott waved him off.

The crowd parted from in front of the car until the massive form of the Reverend Lisa Linton blocked their path. She wore her trademark flowered smock and Coptic gold cross. She pushed long stringy hair from her face and pointed at Ashley.

"They can take everything we own and put us all in jail if they want," she said, "but they cannot silence our hearts. They cannot rob us of our faith. Christ has risen." She shook her fist.

An angry murmur buzzed through the crowd. Picketers shook their signs at Scott's car. He eased off on the brake, letting it roll forward slowly. Linton didn't move.

"Shit!" he said under his breath.

Sirens wailed from far off.

"The gift of life eternal has been granted to us by the Almighty and the United States government is trying to rob us of its glory," Linton screamed. "They can't control the Internet. Too many know the truth."

Scott tapped the horn, making her jump. "You don't get out of my way," he said, "I'll help you find life eternal."

Linton crossed her arms and locked eyes with Ashley. "Go to hell," she said.

Scott dropped the shifter into neutral and stomped on the gas. Linton stumbled backward. Scott put the car back into gear and resumed his slow crawl. Ashley giggled nervously.

Wild-eyed, Linton charged the car, punching the hood while squad cars converged on the scene, causing her to punch harder before uniforms moved in. Two cops grabbed her by each arm. More lined the way in front of Scott's car, pushing the crowd back. An older cop waved them toward the building.

It took four cops to drag Linton off, one under each arm and one on each leg. She kicked and struggled, keeping her eyes riveted to Ashley's the whole time they carried her away.

CHAPTER TWENTY NINE

Ashley followed Scott into the building, peering back over her shoulder in time to see the San Diego Police push Lisa Linton into a van. More cops dispersed the crowd, subduing and cuffing any who resisted. Once inside, they took the elevator and went straight to Relling's office. The receptionist looked up when they approached and surprised Ashley when she punched the intercom, saying, "They're here."

She followed Scott, stopping inside the door when they saw Ken Dawson behind Relling's desk holding up the front page of the morning edition. Relling sat to the side, hands clenched in his lap, looking everywhere but at them. Where was Mossbarger? Ashley wondered.

"Great story," Dawson said to Relling who still wouldn't look at Ashley. Dawson leveled his gaze at her. "Mr. Relling was just telling me about the five million dollar contract his mother's book publishing division is offering for your exposé of the Cyberchurch."

"What?" Scott said.

"We'd like to retain you for three million to edit and consult, Miller," Relling added.

A maelstrom of emotions tumbled through Ashley, making it hard to speak. Dawson pulled a bundle of files from a briefcase. "We have all the research right here. The truth about Justin Stephens and the Cyberchurch cult murders. He and Linton were lovers."

"Say what?" Scott blurted.

"It was a religious scam Stephens cooked up," Dawson said. "He conned Linton and the others into believing his reports and doctored photographs. Not only did he use the Cyberchurch to fleece his followers," Dawson continued, his eyes never leaving Ashley. "His secret inner circle murdered and dismembered Christine Daniels as a sacrifice."

Bill Relling stood, took the files from Dawson and handed them to Ashley. She saw his eyes then. Fear. "We have all the facts right here. Eight million dollars between you and Miller. The research has all been done. All you have to do is write the story."

Ashley looked over at Scott, who remained silent, his way of letting her handle it. "So you want to put your words in my mouth again, pay me off, and forget any of this happened. Is that what I'm hearing?" She looked from Relling's cowering gaze to Dawson.

Both men nodded.

"Forget it," she heard herself say.

Relling's face puckered. "You have to take…"

"I don't have to take anything!"

He sighed. "Either accept our offer and let us take care of you or you're out of a job." He nodded to Scott, who had crossed his arms and leaned on the edge of a table. "You too!"

"Whatever Ashley decides, that's what I do," Scott said.

Ashley looked to Dawson, who stared out the window as if nothing happening here had anything to do with him.

"Take the money or lose my job," she said.

Relling nodded toward Dawson. "Your five million is tax free."

"You're out of your mind if you think I care about the money," Ashley said. "You're trying to buy my name to publish your lies."

Relling's face flushed and his eyes looked as if they were about to jump out of his head.

"You can play your sneaky tricks," she said, turning to leave, "but you can't stop the truth." She walked out, Scott following.

Too easy, she thought looking back when she reached the door. To her surprise, neither Relling or Dawson said more.

"What are we going to do?" Scott said, hurrying to catch her near the elevator.

"I'm making this up as I go," she said, when they stepped in. "We need to clear out of here. We need some time to think."

"You know they'll be watching everything we do."

The elevator stopped at her floor. "What else is new?" She took him by the arm and pulled him close. "I'm scared shit," she whispered.

"They're going to kill us."

A fire alarm klaxon pierced the air, making them jump.

"Jesus," Ashley put her hand to her heart. "Now what?"

Scott led her toward an exit while people spilled from offices. A steady stream of reporters poured through the door from the city room at the end of the hall.

"I don't like this," Ashley said.

"Keep your eyes open." Scott quickened his step and pulled his keys from his pocket. A long-haired teenager wearing baggy pants, a backward baseball cap, sunglasses, and a leather jacket ran into him, almost knocking him over.

"Hey," Scott said, flailing for balance.

The kid grabbed Scott's keys from him and ran off, turning around near the door. "Fuck you!" he said, sticking up both middle fingers.

Scott looked as if he'd been hit in the face. "You little maggot!"

The kid disappeared through the fire exit door with Scott running after him. Ashley followed them through the door. Looking down, she saw the back of the kid's head a couple of flights down. He had a three flight lead by the time they reached the ground floor. Scott and Ashley ran into the parking lot breathless, scanning the crowd for signs of him.

"The little bastard took my keys," Scott muttered.

The picketers were gone. Two cops came across the parking lot and went into the building while the wail of sirens rose in the distance. Ashley turned back to the building looking and smelling for smoke.

"Come on." Scott led her toward the underground parking. "Something is very wrong here. I can feel it. I have a spare key hidden in a magnet box. Let's get out of here."

"No argument from me." She broke into a trot beside him. The sound of their footsteps echoing off the low parking structure ceiling gave her goosebumps. No people down here. They had all gone out the front and back.

Scott retrieved the key from under his car's bumper. Hurrying to get away, they pulled out of the lot past a sea of confused faces. Ashley's tension lightened when they passed through the gate. She felt even better when they pulled into the street.

"Stop the car and get out or I'll blow your brains out," a voice said behind them.

Ashley caught the glint of metal pressed to the back of Scott's neck when she started to look back. "Keep looking straight ahead," the voice said, stopping her.

"I'll only say this once," the kid said. "Put the car into park and step out or I'll cap you right here." He pushed Scott's head forward. "Don't think I won't."

"Do what he says," Ashley said.

Scott grabbed the door handle and eased out of the car. He started to look back when the kid's voice stopped him. "Don't even think about it." He waved Scott away. "Run back to the building."

Ashley's heart beat crazily when the kid moved behind her. He pressed an ether soaked cloth over her nose and mouth while pressing the gun behind her ear. The thought of screaming burst through her mind like a roman candle before fading into darkness with the rest of her.

CHAPTER THIRTY

Something fuzzy bobbed into Ashley's vision, slowly forming into the features of a soft androgynous face. She recognized the eyes first, old and wizened in spite of youthful skin. She blinked for better focus. Chris Daniels. The kid from the email. Confusion fluttered through her like startled birds. This had to be a dream.

Ancient periwinkle blue eyes studied her from beneath big feathery lashes. The tiny crow's feet at their edges added to the sageness of his expression, but his smooth oval face looked feminine. Thin and lanky, he had long, straight honey colored hair parted in the middle, falling over his shoulders. He spun a pair of sunglasses on the end of his finger.

Ashley sat up trying to get her bearings. She still felt woozy.

"Sorry about that cheap carjacking shit," he said in a voice that was obviously male. "I hate those punks, but I didn't know what else to do." He held up a small length of chrome pipe and dropped it onto the bed. "That's my gun."

"Who are you?" she said, feeling stupid for asking.

"Jesus Christ," he said, "If you believe those crazy fucks from the Cyberchurch."

This was crazy. What were Mossbarger and Dawson trying to pull now? She had to get out of here. She started to stand and threw her arm out for balance when she felt dizzy.

Chris stepped forward and gently pushed her back. "Don't bother and don't scream." He put his hands over his ears. "I don't need the headache. You can run if you want, but you won't see anyone for

114

miles." He walked to the window and looked out. "And we'll be out of here before anybody can find us."

She looked around the bedroom. Old fashioned wall paper and light fixtures. A farm house. "Get me out of here," she said louder than she intended.

Chris held up his hands. "The last thing I'm going to do is hurt you and the Doc wouldn't hurt a flea. Give us a little time, that's all. You don't like what you hear, we'll let you walk." He held his hand up in a Boy Scout salute. "Promise."

"How old are you?" she said.

"Physiologically, late thirties. Chronologically, fifteen. My body's supposed to even itself out more in another six months or so."

She breathed in extra slow trying to make sense of it, but his casual attitude made her nervous. "If you are who you say you are," she said more to herself, "then who kidnapped me the first time? Who died?"

Chris's expression darkened and the corners of his mouth turned down. "Killers and liars." The fire in his eyes frightened her. He turned away and looked out the window. When he spoke again, his voice came low and controlled. "That freak that kidnapped you. He was going to rape you, right?"

"Yes," she said softly.

"It was the same bastard that killed my sister. Doc says he's probably one of those CIA commando maniacs."

"They paid a rapist murderer, and then killed him?"

Chris shook his fist. "Served him right. That asshole killed my sister and cut her up. She was my twin. She always wanted to do the right thing. Always talked about being dignified and strong..." His voice trailed off.

Another silence hung between them. Chris stared at the floor red faced while Ashley's heart swelled. "What about you?"

He looked up with narrowed eyes. "I knew I was screwed from the start so I didn't give a shit about anything." He shrugged. "My probation officer says I have a hard time adjusting."

Ashley got up slowly from the bed and went to the other window to look out over a field with a wall of trees on its far side. "Probation officer?"

"Doc Stephens got me out of jail. Some bullshit about having a control for his experiment with my sister. Christine and I were rare Progeria twins. Doc got me out of a three year stretch. Grand larceny.

Driving under the influence. Drug possession. Speaking of which…" He pulled a joint from his pocket and put it to his lips. "Don't mind do you? It settles me down."

"Would it matter if I did?"

Chris shrugged. "Thought I'd be polite and ask." He pulled out a lighter, lit the joint and took a deep hit before offering it to her. "Calms my nerves," he said letting minimal smoke escape.

Ashley declined.

"So they released me into Doc's custody." He blew out smoke. Its smell reminded Ashley of college. "I was going to make a run for it until the Doc told me that he wanted to help Christine."

Outside, Ashley saw metal glinting in the distance, then a car. "Someone's coming."

"Shit." Chris tapped the joint out in his palm, hurried to the window and opened it, fanning the room. "Don't tell Doc I was smoking weed. He'll get pissed." He tucked the partially smoked joint into a baggie, which he rolled up and stuffed into his pocket. "You're the only hope we have. Please listen to what the Doc says."

She heard the crunch of gravel as the car pulled around to the far side of the house, then a door slammed followed by footsteps.

"Remember what I said," Chris whispered. "Don't say anything about the weed." The front door opened and closed and the footsteps came closer. She heard a key in the lock before the bedroom door swung open.

CHAPTER THIRTY ONE

A thin, middle-aged sandy haired man came into the room, his pointed nose lifted and sniffing. He frowned at Chris from behind wire rimmed glasses before turning to Ashley. "I apologize for all the barbaric subterfuge," he said with an Oxford accent.

No, it can't be, Ashley thought. No way. I'm not buying this.

He held out his hand and shook hers. "Justin Stephens."

He bowed slightly and sat in a chair by the window, crossed his legs, and clasped his hands over his knee. From this angle, his drawn face and short beard accented his angular features. "It was Chris's idea," he continued. "I was against it, but he did it anyway." He turned to Chris, who leaned against the wall with his arms crossed, a smirk playing at the corner of his mouth.

"I have to admit," Stephens said, shaking his head. "It was very clever in spite of its uncouthness."

Chris straightened. "I told you, stick with me Doc and I'll show you how it's done."

"You'll also show me the way to jail if you don't get me killed first."

Chris smiled.

"And don't think I can't smell your marijuana. You know I disapprove of it."

Chris waved the older man off with a half-hearted gesture.

"You're Justin Stephens?" Ashley said, feeling stupid for voicing the obvious.

He sighed. "I apologize for our desperate actions, but Mossbarger and Dawson are ruthless." He looked to Chris again.

The mention of Mossbarger and Dawson quickened Ashley's heart beat. How did she know this wasn't another engineered situation? "I think you need to take me back to San Diego," she said.

Stephens nodded. "In due time and not until after dark. We've already risked too much. I'm hoping you'll dine with us. I've brought some Mexican food. Chris's favorite. We have quite a story to tell you. If you will listen, I give you my word that when I finish you will be free to choose your own course of action."

"I've heard lines like that before."

"Doc gives his word, that's serious shit." Chris started toward the door.

"I told you to watch your language around ladies," Stephens said, a note of reproach in his voice.

"Sorry Doc."

Stephens held out his hand and bowed to Ashley. "Shall we?"

In spite of the surrealness of her situation, Ashley felt less and less threatened by this odd pair with each passing moment. She followed Chris out of the room with Stephens behind her. The three of them went down a hall, through a small room to a dining area.

"It's in the kitchen," Stephens said. "Chris, for once in your life, be a gentleman and get our dinner."

"Yessuh massuh." Chris bowed and went to the kitchen.

"And something to drink," Stephens said.

"Why did you pick me for your email?" Ashley said, taking the chair beside him.

He stroked his beard. "Your article on the rain forest activists caught my eye." He shook his finger. "Excellent piece. If anybody could get to the truth, I knew you could." He lowered his voice. "But I had no right putting you in danger."

His praise flattered her and unless he was a brilliant actor, Ashley sensed his sincerity. She remembered how she had been cornered and trapped and understood the hopelessness of having no place to turn. "I know how you feel," she said, feeling her throat tighten at the words. "Two of my best friends are gone."

"They did the same with my life long friend, my colleagues, my life's work, and Chris's sister, God rest her soul." He bowed his head. "Close to two dozen people have vanished." He looked up, a faraway look in his eyes. "Frank Forte, Alice Rondeau, Terry Hinchliffe, Margaret Dunbar, interns, support staff -- all gone along with my lab, computers, equipment, and records."

Ashley's breath caught, her face flushed and hot tears ran down her cheeks. "My God, Jeff, Rob…"

"Gone," Stephens said in a monotone. "Just like my staff."

His pained expression left Ashley with no doubt of his sadness and loss. No one could act *this* good. Chris came back with paper plates, napkins and a white bag of Mexican fast food.

"Tell me what happened," she said after a few bites of a burrito. "I have no idea who or what to believe. I might as well listen to you."

"That's why we brought you here." Stephens looked to Chris. "I've turned off Chris's aging gene and it's brought nothing but death to anyone who's had anything to do with it. If it weren't for you and those Cyberchurch people, no trace of my discovery would have survived." He shook his head. "My young friend here is far from Jesus Christ, believe me. He has a criminal record as long as my arm."

Chris's face flushed.

"What about your sister?" Ashley said.

"She was an angel," Stephens said. "The most selfless and giving person I ever met."

"Goody two shoes," Chris muttered. "Look where it got her."

"Enough of that!" Stephens shook a finger at Chris, who dropped his head.

"Sorry Doc, it pisses me off every time I think about it."

Stephens sighed.

"Growing up knowing I'm two steps from dead pissed me off," Chris said, sipping his drink. "I didn't give a shit about anything. Someone has a nice car? I take it. Whatever I want, whenever I want it, as long as it looks like I have a clean shot at it." He tapped his chest. "No one's taking it with them. They're all going to croak just like me only not as fast, so I figured I might as well enjoy it for the short time I'm here."

"What about now?" Ashley said. "If you're immortal like Dr. Stephens says, your attitude should be different."

Chris frowned.

"Now you've heard it from someone besides me," Stephens added.

"That's all fine and dandy, but look what they did to my sister." Chris said, bitterness seeping through his words.

Ashley shook off a chill, remembering how close she had come to the same fate.

CHAPTER THIRTY TWO

C hris cleared the table and the three of them went to a den at the front of the house where oil paintings of wilderness settings hung on two of the walls. Outside the sun had fallen, leaving a pink tinged horizon behind the trees. Chris took a rocking chair in one corner and Stephens sat in a stuffed chair beside the window, leaving Ashley the couch on the far wall. Though Chris and Stephens were too bizarre to be real, she sensed no deception from them, only sincerity to the point of brutal honesty from Chris.

"Who owns this place?" she said, sitting back on the couch.

"A good friend," Stephens answered. "I won't mention his name. I have too many deaths on my conscience as it is."

"If everything you've told me were to be true," Ashley said, kicking her shoes off and stretching out on the couch. "How did you survive? If everyone else connected with whatever the hell you did is gone. For all I know, I'm vanished now too."

Stephens shook his head. "Only if you want to be. Once I tell my story you're free to act as you see fit." He looked over at Chris who rocked back and forth in his chair, arms crossed, listening. "As much as I hate to admit it," Stephens continued. "If it weren't for Chris' flagrant disregard for the law, we wouldn't be talking right now. He'd gotten himself arrested that afternoon. I was getting him out of jail when they hit."

"It was a beautiful Porsche Boxster," Chris said. "With the keys in it screaming, 'Steal me!'"

"I was in the middle of some tests on Christine at Genengineering,"

Stephens said. "When I got a call from the San Diego Police. They had Chris under arrest for driving a stolen car around the track at Madison high school." He glanced at Chris, frowning. "During a football game."

Chris smiled sheepishly. "I would have gotten away with it if they hadn't put an ambulance in front of me. I didn't want to hurt anybody." He shook his head. "I was just giving them a little entertainment."

"I was so intent on my tests with Christine," Stephens said, waving Chris off, "that I didn't even know he had gone out. I was preparing to present the results of my research at a conference that weekend. I should have released my findings when I had my first successes with lower organisms," he said half to himself.

"How could you try your experiments on humans so quickly? I don't mean to come across judgmental, but it seems a bit cavalier."

Stephens nodded toward Chris. "Chris and Christine were rare Progeroid twins that gave me a perfect set of controls. Christine was a straight A student. Chris was a hellion who hacked the schools computers, changed everyone's grades, and transferred the school staff's payroll deductions from the United Way to the National Organization for the Reformation of Marijuana Laws. That day they caught him in a stolen car with a bag of marijuana. He swallowed six doses of LSD right after they discovered the pot."

"Eight," Chris said. "You know what it's like to fry in a jail cell with a bunch of idiots looking in on you like a caged monkey?"

"It doesn't sound like a situation I would ever get myself into," Ashley said. "Where were your parents?"

Chris looked to Stephens, who continued. "Chris never knew his father. We think he might have been in the Navy. His mother left them the day after they were born. No one came for them so they became wards of the state."

"Which wasn't any better than the slam," Chris added. "Who wants a freak?"

"Enough of that." Stephens leaned toward the window and stared out at the coming night. "When Chris was arrested this last time he called me and they released him to me. It was Chris who noticed two men following us back to Genengineering,"

"I spotted them as soon as we got in the car." Chris chuckled. "Doc wouldn't believe me until I had him drive around in a circle. We lost them in the parking lot at Scripps Institute and ran inside to a private lounge where Doc borrowed a friend's car." Chris pointed at Stephens. "He's a sly old dog. Faked 'em all out!"

Stephens turned back from the window. "We drove by the lab later that night. They had the entrance blocked off and a row of trucks in front of it."

"Suits everywhere," Chris said.

"Loading up the trucks and tearing out the fixtures," Stephens added. "They took everything. Books, notes, experiments, lab equipment, files, my entire staff…"

"And my sister," Chris growled.

No one spoke. The chirp of crickets drifted in from the darkness. Ashley felt trapped, far outside the mainstream, as if some faceless monster would spring on her the moment she showed herself.

"I kept a copy of all my notes and research on my laptop," Stephens said, breaking their silence. "It's the written proof of my accomplishment. I sent you the theoretical notes I had prepared for my presentation. This is the real proof and Chris is the only living proof."

And I'm hiding out with you in an old house in the middle of nowhere, Ashley thought. Stuck with you and the question of life and death. She closed her eyes, struggling to understand everything. "How did? I mean what if?" She looked up at their expectant faces. "You're putting this in my lap, aren't you?"

They both nodded.

She leaned forward and put her face in her hands. "Who the hell did I piss off?"

CHAPTER THIRTY THREE

"It's dark now," Stephens said. "Your car is in the garage. You're free to go."

Ashley glanced at Chris whose gaze stayed on her.

"You are also welcome to stay. The room is made up for you."

"Can I call Scott? Let him know I'm all right?"

"I'm sorry, but contact is unacceptable. You've seen what they can do." He motioned with his head for Chris to follow him. "Let's leave Miss Butler alone so she can rest and gather her thoughts."

"Thank you," Ashley said, not knowing what else to say.

"I need your word," Stephens said, his gaze pinning her, "that if you leave, you will let us know so we can get away."

"I promise."

"Good enough, then." He stood. "Can I get you anything more?"

"I'd like to write a letter to Scott. He needs to know I'm all right."

"I understand. Chris, be a gentleman and get Miss Butler a pen and paper."

Chris snapped to attention and saluted. "Sir, yes sir." He spun on his heels and left.

"He's really not a bad kid," Stephens said conspiratorially, after Chris left the room. "Lots of anger, but he wouldn't hurt anyone. Even though he'd never admit it, he respects what I tell him. It's himself he doesn't respect." Stephens tapped his forehead with his finger and whispered. "He questions everything. Drives me out of my mind sometimes." He smiled wryly.

Chris returned with the writing supplies. "I'm upstairs Miss Butler.

You need anything, just shout."

"Thanks." She took the pen and paper and went back to the room she had awakened in a few short hours ago. Sitting with pillows at her back, she propped a book on her knees for a desk and put pen to paper.

Dear Scott,

I am free to come and go as I please, but I need to stay away awhile. I can't tell you where I am or who I am with because I don't want to put you in danger.

If anyone else reads this, they will know that you know nothing. They will also expect me to contact you again. You're their only connection to me. Promise that you will do nothing except your job. If they think they might find me through you, it will keep you safe. When the time is right and I am sure it is safe, I will contact you, but it could be days, weeks, or months. Maybe years. I hate leaving you in the dark like this, but it is for your own safety. Stay well.

Love Ashley

She reread the letter before putting it in an envelope, addressing it, and leaving it on the nightstand. She turned off the light and closed her eyes thinking of the grief and loss that filtered through everything Justin Stephens said and did, then she thought of her own losses and felt her emotions spinning out of control. Jeff Hamilton. Gone. Rob… Tears fell until her grief dragged her down into unconsciousness, the only escape she could find.

CHAPTER THIRTY FOUR

She opened her eyes to darkness some time later, feeling as if she hadn't slept. The pillow beneath was wet from her tears. She stared at the ceiling trying to puzzle through it all. Someone padded down the hall past her door toward the front of the house. When the footsteps didn't return, Ashley kicked back the covers, pulled on her jeans and blouse and crept out of the room. Running her hand down the wall in the semi-darkness, she fumbled her way to the front of the house where she found Justin Stephens by the window, staring out into the night.

"All I wanted to do was save the children," he said without turning around. "Give them their lives back. Now I'm hunted like an animal." He sighed. "Chris kidnapped you because I feared for your life." He turned toward her, his features shadowed in the darkness. "I reached out to you because I had nowhere else to turn and now my selfishness has cost you."

"It had to be someone," Ashley said, reaching for the words to comfort him with. "It might as well have been me."

He turned back to the night. "I never thought the power of God would be thrust into my hands like this. I never intended to open Pandora's Box."

Ashley listened, not speaking for fear of stopping him from unburdening. If she had any doubts before now, his gestures, thoughts, and the timbre of his voice all convinced her that he had in fact discovered immortality.

"Pandora's box," he said, shaking his head. "It always comes back to the archetypal myths, doesn't it? I called my initial discovery the

Methuselah effect." He held his hands out, speaking to the darkness as if it were his confessor. "It's the genetic equivalence of alchemical transmutation; the belief that turning base metals into gold held the secret of immortality, only now it's new genes for old. Do you know the saddest part of all this madness?" He waited a few beats, then, "The government is right. If we become immortal and continue to reproduce, we seal our doom by outstripping our resources. The only way to survive would be to exterminate ourselves to ease the crowding. Who would live? Who would die? Who decides?" He put his head in his hands. "If there is a God, what is he telling us?"

"That we can't have life without death."

Ashley's words hung between them until the other side of it tugged at her. What would it be like to live eternally? How much could you learn? How far could you develop yourself?

"And then there's Chris," Stephens said, getting her attention again. "I have no right to take his life. That choice is his. He wants a gun so he can leave this life the way he chooses. I'm trying to talk him into something more peaceful. Euthanasia. Pills. Chris insists that he make that choice on his own terms in his own way. Right now he's determined to make it as messy as possible." Stephens turned from the window to look into Ashley's eyes, then he dropped into the easy chair. "So here we are. Keepers of fate."

"What about you?" Ashley said. "Have you thought about what it would be like to continue your research into eternity?"

"I think about Chris," Stephens said. "I can't take his life and I can't allow anyone else to take it either. Is it right for him to live forever alone?"

Ashley had no answer.

Stephens stood. "I'll be right back," he said, leaving the room. He returned a few minutes later with a briefcase. Sitting in his chair, he opened it in his lap and spun it toward her. Two pairs of syringes, one large, the other smaller, and two pairs of small bottles sat snuggled into form fit cut outs in egg crate foam.

"The smaller syringes are for a powerful local anesthetic. The bigger ones have to go deep into the bone."

"Two more treatments," she said.

"Chris needs a family."

"You're not suggesting…"

He held a hand up. "I'm not suggesting anything. I don't know that

I have the nerve to do it myself. If I do, and I ever desire death, I will have to kill myself." He looked up, his eyes penetrating hers. "Chris has that responsibility now. I gave it to him. I don't know if I can bear it myself."

He closed the lid and put the case beside his chair. "All I want is to do the right thing, only I don't know what that is. We all have to make our own choices. I would never force one on anyone else. I didn't mean to with Chris. I certainly never would with you."

CHAPTER THIRTY FIVE

After Stephens packed up his briefcase and went back to bed, Ashley lay awake in her room thinking about the responsibility he had shared with her. Whatever path Chris took and however long he chose to follow it, he carried his end with him. She couldn't fathom what it would be like to be born under a short-term death sentence, then be given control over your own death. Forever.

She looked out the window at the first indigo tinge of the rising sun rimming the horizon. A bird chirped, signaling the coming day. What was happening out there? Scott had to be worried sick. Ashley closed her eyes and drifted toward sleep.

Sunlight filled the room when she opened her eyes again. She heard Chris and Stephens in another part of the house. She climbed out of bed to see what was happening. She found them watching television in the front room.

"Good timing," Chris said when she came in. "The news is on next. From what I saw on the previews, you and I are stars."

Ashley groaned and curled up on the far end of the couch. After a commercial for the San Diego Wild Animal Park, the news started.

"In our top story," a blonde older woman said, "A Cyberchurch rally erupted in violence for the second time in as many weeks."

Behind her, scenes from a confrontation between police and Cyberchurch members played out in the *San Diego Times* parking lot.

"IRS agents arrested the Reverend Lisa Linton for tax fraud and seized the Cyberchurch's assets."

Behind the announcer, a sequence of scenes flashed showing raids at various locations.

"After a series of bizarre events revolving around a hoax that many believed to be the second coming of Christ in cyberspace, a tangled drama has emerged, involving church and state battling over religious freedom on the Internet. Have you seen him?" the blonde announcer said.

A blowup of Chris filled the screen behind her.

"Not this shit again." Chris waved away the screen.

"Have you seen me? flyers have been circulating all over San Diego and the Internet," she continued. "All searching for what federal agents call a mythical being. In the midst of the confusion, Ashley Butler, the reporter who first broke the story, has disappeared."

The unflattering clip of Ashley being escorted from the kidnapper's house with Mossbarger filled the screen.

"Channel Eight and the San Diego Times have posted a twenty five thousand dollar reward for information leading to Ashley's safe return. A special hot line has been set up."

A phone number scrolled across the screen while Ashley's picture cut to a shot of Scott surrounded by reporters and microphones.

"Earlier this week," a woman's voice said. "Ashley was kidnapped by a killer who has since been linked to the church. Now she has disappeared. As her editor, do you have any speculation about what might have happened to her?"

"All I know is that we want her back safe." Scott's face looked drawn and pale. Dark circles ringed his eyes. "Please be on the alert for any sign of her or any suspicious activity. That's all I have to say for now. It's in the hands of the police."

"In a formal statement from her jail cell," the announcer continued. "Reverend Linton accused the federal government of being tools of the antichrist who staged the Cyberchurch riots to put an end to the second coming." An unattractive picture of Lisa Linton filled the screen. "In what could be the strangest turn of events, the Cyberchurch's web site, which had been shut down by the United States government has been duplicated all over the world, with each of those having dozens of proxy websites."

A world map, populating itself with red dots came on the screen.

"They are all linking to each other through hypertext links," the announcer continued, "making what is in effect, one giant website." She paused, then "This phenomena has given credence to the eerily prescient comments made by Linton who had predicted this. Here in the United States, the Internal Revenue Service is deluged with requests for new churches requesting tax-free status. Requests are presently coming in three times faster than they can be processed."

"I'll be damned," Ashley said.

"In the mean time," the announcer said as riot scenes from different parts of the world played on screens behind her. "Demonstrations have broken out all over Europe, protesting the actions of the United States government against the Cyberchurch."

The camera panned back. "Stay tuned for weather and sports after a short break," she said.

Chris picked up the remote and clicked the television off.

"Those halfwits who think I'm Jesus are in for a big disappointment," he said.

"Don't worry, Chris," Stephens said. "You're the furthest thing from Jesus anyone could imagine. I have a copy of your rap sheet to prove it. One of the things to think about," Stephens said, turning to Ashley, "is what you want to do when Chris and I leave." He held her gaze. "Just as you are free to leave whenever you wish, you are welcome to come with us."

She glanced over to see Chris, who studied her with his own questioning expression.

CHAPTER THIRTY SIX

The three of them spent the better part of the day trying to ferret the truth out of what they saw and heard on television. The afternoon news repeated the morning's segment. The government was trying unsuccessfully to dismantle the Cyberchurch. Ashley had no doubt that they were frantically searching for her, Chris, and Doctor Stephens. As the day drew to a close, sunlight streamed through the window, bathing the front room where they had spent most of the day in warm gold. Chris had gone upstairs to take a nap.

Stephens leaned back in the easy chair and crossed his arms. "As much as you and I hate it," he said, "the government is right. We can't allow the populace exposure to this curse."

"We can't give away the secret," Ashley said, "but we can give them facts about what's happened."

"What will that accomplish?"

Her heartbeat quickened. "I'm talking about the freedom to choose. The freedom to speak. The government stole my work and wrote their lies with my name on them. Lies about you. Your work. The people have a right to know."

"Unless you're silenced first."

"I'm willing to die trying."

Stephens graced her with a lopsided smile. "Death. That's the real quandary, isn't it? Who lives and who dies? We are designed by God to die. Accident, famine, war, disease, or old age. It's only a matter of when." He leaned forward, keeping her gaze. "Death is the only true reality," he said, sounding chillingly rational. "The choice has been thrust on us. On Chris. It's quite a responsibility." His eyes softened. "Chris has been carrying it alone. Because of me. I have to take the responsibility." He pulled a medical bag from beside his chair and opened it, showing her bottles and bottles of pills.

"There are many ways to go," he said, closing the bag. "Right now I must share the load. My load that Chris has been carrying."

"You're going to inject yourself?"

Stephens reached beside him again and came up with a laptop computer. "I'm not sure what to do with this. It has all my work on it. If they find us they'll get it." He tapped the computer. "If they get it, it's guaranteed that someone will unleash the plague."

"Why don't you hide it?"

"I'm considering that. I'm also debating on whether to give it to you."

"I'm not so sure I want it," Ashley said.

He smiled. "We all have to make our own choices." He rose and crossed the room, putting his hand to her cheek in a fatherly gesture. "We all have to respect each other's freedom." He gently lifted her chin with his fingers to look her in the eye. "It's up to us to decide what is best for ourselves." His gaze lingered, then he grabbed his computer and medical bag. "If you'll excuse me, I have some thinking to do."

He left her alone with the red sun of dusk blazing through the window, washing the room in crimson.

CHAPTER THIRTY SEVEN

Ashley sat alone in the darkness of the front room long past the setting of the sun. Her thoughts spiraled into the night, refusing to make choices over issues she couldn't fathom. At some point she closed her eyes, quickly dropping into sleep.

It surprised her when she awoke to the first gray of a new day. How long had she slept? She saw Justin Stephens' computer by her feet, an envelope with her name on it taped to its top. She pulled the envelope off the computer, pulling the screen up with it. Keyboard keys spilled out.

"What the hell is going on?" she muttered.

On closer inspection she saw that the screen had been smashed and the case cracked and broken. The hard drive lay on top, its components broken, the disk itself gone. She pulled the envelope from the screen and opened it. A note in precise printing had been tucked inside. She unfolded it and started reading in the growing light of day.

Dear Ashley,

Forgive me for leaving this way, but this is the safest course of action. I let Chris do the honors with the computer. It's good for him to get his anger out.

My discovery lives safe in my mind, in Chris, and in my body now too. I will be gone with Chris by the time you read this. He and I have both dreamed of traveling through Mexico, Central and South America, China,

Europe, Africa, New Zealand, and other places. Who knows where we will go first. We plan to study all of humanity.

We loved having you visit. You brought a welcome feminine influence to our lives. Chris's mother died when he was born and his sister was murdered. He thinks very much of you. We talked it over and we didn't want you to think us rude hosts by running out and abandoning you, but we know how much you wanted to write your story. Being good hosts, we left something for you in the kitchen.

Ashley hurried back to the sunlit kitchen where she spotted a note on the table beside what looked like a place setting. Moving as though in a dream, she picked up the note and read.

Ashley:

Take as much time as you need to think about everything. If you decide to join us, you'll have plenty of time to find us.
Do what you think is right.
We'll be in touch very soon.

Much love,

Chris and Justin

The phone rang, startling her. Her knees buckled and the note slipped from her fingers, falling on the small and large syringe and bottle of pills that had been arranged on the table.

ABOUT THE AUTHOR

Matthew J. Pallamary's historical novel of first contact between shamans and Jesuits in 18th century South America, titled, *Land Without Evil*, was published in hard cover by Charles Publishing, and has received rave reviews along with a San Diego Book Award for mainstream fiction. It was chosen as a Reading Group Choices selection. *Land Without Evil* was also adapted into a full-length stage and sky show, co-written by Agent Red with Matt Pallamary, directed by Agent Red, and performed by Sky Candy, an Austin Texas aerial group. The making of the show was the subject of a PBS series, Arts in Context episode, which garnered an EMMY nomination. *Land Without Evil* is in development as a feature film.

His nonfiction book, *The Infinity Zone: A Transcendent Approach to Peak Performance* is a collaboration with professional tennis coach Paul Mayberry which offers a fascinating exploration of the phenomenon that occurs at the nexus of perfect form and motion, bringing balance, power, and coordination to physical and mental activities. *The Infinity Zone* took 1ˢᵗ place in the International Book Awards, Nonfiction, New Age category, and was a finalist in the San Diego Book Awards

His first book, a short story collection titled *The Small Dark Room*

Of The Soul was noted in The Year's Best Horror and Fantasy.

It's follow up *A Short Walk to the Other Side* was an International Book Award Finalist.

Dreamland, a novel about computer generated dreaming, written with Ken Reeth won an Independent e-Book Award in the Horror/Thriller category.

Matt's work has appeared in Oui, New Dimensions, The Iconoclast, Starbright, Infinity, Passport, The Short Story Digest, Redcat, The San Diego Writer's Monthly, Connotations, Phantasm, Essentially You, The Haven Journal, and many others. His fiction has been featured in The San Diego Union Tribune which he has also reviewed books for, and his work has been heard on KPBS-FM in San Diego, KUCI FM in Irvine, KX 93.5 in Laguna Beach, television Channel Three in Santa Barbara, and The Susan Cameron Block Show in Vancouver.

He has been a guest on the following nationally syndicated talk shows; Paul Rodriguez, In The Light with Michelle Whitedove, Susun Weed, Medicine Woman, Inner Journey with Greg Friedman, and Environmental Directions Radio series. Matt has also appeared on the following television shows; Bridging Heaven and Earth, Elyssa's Raw and Wild Food Show, Things That Matter, Literary Gumbo, Indie Authors TV, and ECONEWS. He has also been a frequent guest on numerous podcasts, among them, The Psychedelic Salon, and C-Realm.

He has taught fiction workshops at the Southern California Writers' Conference in San Diego, Palm Springs, and Los Angeles, and at the Santa Barbara Writers' Conference for twenty five years. He has also lectured at the Greater Los Angeles Writer's Conference, the Getting It Write conference in Oregon, the Saddleback Writers' Conference, the Rio Grande Writers' Seminar, the National Council of Teachers of English, The San Diego Writer's and Editor's Guild, The San Diego Book Publicists, The Pacific Institute for Professional Writing, and he has been a panelist at the World Fantasy Convention, Con-Dor, and Coppercon. He is presently Editor in Chief of Muse Harbor Publishing.

Matt also received the Man of the Year 2000 from San Diego Writer's

Monthly Magazine. His memoir *Spirit Matters*, which details his journeys to Peru, working with shamanic plant medicines took first place in the San Diego Book Awards Spiritual Book Category, and was an Award-Winning Finalist in the autobiography/memoir category of the National Best Book Awards, sponsored by USA Book News. *Spirit Matters* is also available as an audio book.

Matt frequently visits the jungles, mountains, and deserts of North, Central, and South America pursuing his studies of shamanism and ancient cultures.

WWW.MATTPALLAMARY.COM

BOOKS BY MATTHEW J. PALLAMARY

THE SMALL DARK ROOM OF THE SOUL

LAND WITHOUT EVIL

SPIRIT MATTERS

DREAMLAND (WITH KEN REETH)

THE INFINITY ZONE (WITH PAUL MAYBERRY)

A SHORT WALK TO THE OTHER SIDE

EYE OF THE PREDATOR

PHANTASTIC FICTION

NIGHT WHISPERS